ISLAND JEOPARDY!

Lisa could see the rider clutching at her horse's mane and realized that the rider had lost control of the reins. They had slipped over her horse's head and there was no way she could reach them. Without the reins to still him, the terrified horse ran wild!

He took off like a flash, speeding past the schooling ring where Lisa was riding. A horse as scared as that could run for a long time, and on an island formed from volcanoes there were a lot of places he could get into trouble. Lisa was barely aware of the riding instructor's dash for her own horse. The only thing she really knew was that she might be the only one who could save the rider from a real disaster.

Her eyes flashed to the schooling ring gate, now so carefully latched. There was no time for gates.

As quickly as she knew how, Lisa turned Jasper around and aimed him for the fence. . . .

THE SADDLE CLUB

Sea Horse

BONNIE BRYANT

A BANTAM SKYLARK BOOK®

NEW YORK · TORONTO · LONDON · SYDNEY · AUCKLAND

I would like to express my special thanks
to Arlene deStrulle of the New York
Aquarium for her help to me.
—B.B.

RL 5, 009–012

SEA HORSE
A Bantam Skylark Book / January 1991

Bantam Books are published by Bantam Books, a division of Bantam Double-
day Dell Publishing Group, Inc. Its trademark, consisting of the words
"Bantam Books" and the portrayal of a rooster, is Registered in U.S. Patent
and Trademark Office and in other countries. Marca Registrada. Bantam
Books, 666 Fifth Avenue, New York, New York 10103.

PRINTED IN THE UNITED STATES OF AMERICA

CWO   0 9 8 7 6 5 4 3 2 1

For Bill Gucker, a/k/a Gooch

1

"WHAT DO YOU think? Should I go swimming or riding first when we get to the resort on San Marco?" thirteen-year-old Lisa Atwood asked her friends as she hefted a saddle off its rack. She was getting ready to tack up a horse before their riding class.

"Riding," her two best friends answered at the same time. That made all three of them laugh. Lisa and her friends, Stevie Lake and Carole Hanson, were three very different people, but there was one thing they agreed on: Horses and horseback riding came first wherever they were.

"What time does your plane leave tomorrow?" Stevie asked.

Lisa's surprise Christmas present from her parents was a trip with them to the Caribbean. As far as Lisa was concerned, the best part about it was the horseback riding offered at the resort.

"We leave at nine-thirty in the morning," Lisa replied. "I should be on the beach by four o'clock. That includes a quick stop at the stables to sign up, of course."

"Of course." Carole grinned happily. "And by then, I'll already have been riding for three hours." Her friends nearly groaned with envy. Carole's Christmas present had been her very own horse. He was a big, beautiful bay gelding with a lopsided star on his forehead. She had named him Starlight. For the rest of her vacation, Carole intended to ride Starlight as much as she could. "It'll be work, though," she reminded Lisa and Stevie. "Starlight really isn't done with his training, and training a horse is hard work."

"Yeah, right, just like lying on the beach is hard work," Stevie said. "Think of all the work you have to do to get your tan just the right shade. I'm the one who really has a lot of work to do in the next week. I have to find a dress for the New Year's Eve dance!"

"Oh, no!" Lisa said, pretending to sound terribly concerned. "Poor Stevie. You'll have to spend so much time at the mall trying on beautiful dresses, and we all know what a terrible chore that is. And then at the dance you'll have to spend hour after hour dancing with Phil Marston right up until the New Year. It sounds pretty awful." Lisa giggled. "I wonder what I'll be doing at midnight. I think I'll be thinking about you. Hey, do you guys believe in ESP?" Stevie and Carole shrugged dubiously. "Well," Lisa continued, "at midnight, we are all going to be apart, but maybe, if we think of one another at the same moment, it will be like being together."

"Sure," Stevie said, catching on, "this could be an experiment. If it works, maybe we'll get written up in some textbook."

"It would be more fun if we could just be together," Lisa said.

"I don't know," Stevie said. "I like you guys just fine, and at midnight on New Year's Eve, I promise to think of you—a little—but I'm looking forward to being with Phil."

"It's a tough job," Carole said brightly, "but somebody's got to do it. And, speaking of tough jobs, Max asked if we could mix up some grain in a winter blend after class. Can you two stick around?" Stevie and Lisa willingly agreed. It might be the last chance the three of them would have to be together until Lisa got back from her vacation.

The Max Carole mentioned was Max Regnery, the owner of Pine Hollow Stables, where the three girls had met and become friends. They had riding classes together twice a week and Pony Club meetings there every Saturday. Pine Hollow was also the place where Carole's horse, Starlight, lived. Sometimes their families thought the horse-crazy girls lived there, too! The three friends loved horses and horseback riding so much that they had formed their own group, The Saddle Club. The club had simple requirements for membership. First of all, members had to be horse crazy, and second of all, they had to be willing to help one another out. Sometimes the helping had to do with horses and sometimes it had to do with other things, like schoolwork. Whatever it was, when a friend needed help, The Saddle Club came to the rescue.

The P.A. system buzzed to life. "Class in ten minutes," came the familiar voice of Max's mother, universally called Mrs. Reg.

"Yipes, and we've still got to tack up!" Carole cried, grabbing Starlight's saddle and bridle. "See you in the ring!"

With that, she shot out of the tack room to Starlight's stall. Lisa and Stevie weren't far behind her.

Lisa was still huffing as she hoisted Pepper's saddle and settled it onto the horse's back. Tacking up a horse usually took only a few minutes, but that was almost more time than she had. Max was pretty relaxed about most things, but when it came to horses, he was as strict as could be. That included being on time for his classes.

As soon as Pepper's saddle girth was tightened, Lisa climbed onto her horse and proceeded as quickly as possible to the indoor ring, where her class was to take place. She only paused to brush the stable's good-luck horseshoe, posted by the large doorway. That was one of Pine Hollow's many traditions, for no rider who had touched the horseshoe had ever gotten seriously hurt riding.

"Whew!" Lisa sighed to herself when she found that the class had not yet been called to order. She brought Pepper out into the ring and proceeded to walk him in circles as a warm-up.

"Miss Atwood?" Max asked. Lisa didn't like the sound of his words. He never called anybody Miss or Mr. unless something was wrong.

"Yes, Mr. Regnery?" she asked nervously.

"Haven't you forgotten something?" he asked.

Lisa looked down at Pepper. Before she spotted the problem, she heard the titters. One of her classmates—one she vowed never to talk to again—even pointed. It took Lisa a second to see her mistake.

Lisa could feel herself flush. She'd been in such a hurry to put on Pepper's saddle that she'd completely forgotten about his bridle. The horse was still wearing his halter and a lead rope.

"I—uh—" she began. She didn't have the faintest idea what to say. She was so embarrassed, she didn't even know what to do.

"Nice job!" Stevie said, approaching her. "Here's the bridle now." Stevie slipped Pepper's bit into his mouth and brought the bridle up over his head. She fastened the buckle, handed the reins to Lisa, and talked to Max the whole time. "Wasn't Lisa doing a good job, Max?" she asked. "It's so important for a horse to learn to respond to leg signals and when Lisa suggested that it would be a good exercise to work without a bridle for a while, well, I wasn't sure she was ready for that, but she was sensational, wasn't she? Pepper did everything she asked!"

For a few seconds, Max just looked at Stevie. An amused look crossed his face. Stevie could be so outrageous. Everybody knew that. But right then, Lisa and Max knew that what she was being was a friend.

5

"Yes, nice work, Lisa," he said. "Now, would you like to try riding the usual way?"

"Of course," Lisa said. She untwisted Pepper's reins and twined the leather around her fingers properly. By the time she was ready, Carole had also entered the ring, and class began.

"WHAT WAS GOING on in there?" Carole asked later when the three girls met after class in the feed-storage room. "I mean, I thought Max was going to blast me for being late, but there you were, just adjusting your reins when I got there."

"It's a long story," Stevie said.

"But it's worth telling," Lisa added.

"And it's got to be worth hearing, too. Whatever it was, you guys saved me from getting a lecture from Max."

"And Stevie saved me from worse," Lisa said. Then, with a lot of help from Stevie, she told Carole about her mistake and Stevie's clever rescue.

"Do you think Max actually believed you?" Carole asked.

"I don't know," Lisa said dubiously.

"Not for a minute," Stevie said, confirming Lisa's suspicions. "He knew it was a whopper, but there wasn't any reason for you to be laughed at."

"I guess that's just one more thing to love about Max," Lisa said.

"Are you girls going to talk or work?" Max asked, startling all three of them at once. They hadn't even heard him open the door. Lisa wondered briefly if he'd heard what she'd just said. Then she decided very sensibly that she didn't have to think about that because she'd been embarrassed enough for one day.

"Work," Carole said earnestly. "As soon as you tell us what it is we're supposed to do."

Max showed them what he wanted. There were four bags of grain that he wanted mixed up. Two bags contained a brand the horses were being fed now. Two bags were a new brand he wanted to get the horses used to. But changing feed could be tricky, so he wanted the girls to make four different blends, gradually changing from mostly old feed to mostly new.

With that information delivered, Max left them to their own devices. As far as Lisa was concerned right then, one of the things *not* to love about Max was his utter confidence in their ability to solve a complicated problem.

"I say we just dump all the feed out on the ground and begin mixing it together," Stevie said, reaching to open the first bag.

"No way!" Carole said. "We have to measure."

"Sure, okay, measure," Stevie conceded. "But measure what? And how?"

Both girls looked at Lisa. Lisa was a straight-A student at school. This was something she'd probably be good at.

Carole sighed. "This is like one of those dumb problems where the store has cashews for three dollars and fifty cents a pound and peanuts for a dollar-fifty a pound and if they sell three pounds of blended nuts—"

"I know the one, and the answer is that the customer

should mix them when he gets home. Or better still, don't blend them. Cashews are much better by themselves," Stevie declared.

"I agree, but that's never on the answer sheet," Lisa said. "So here's what we do." She pulled a piece of paper and a pencil out of her backpack and began scribbling furiously. She scratched out some numbers and put in new ones while Carole and Stevie waited patiently.

"Got it!" she said at last. "Bag one will be one part new feed, five parts old. Bag two will be two parts new, four parts old. Bag three will be four new, two old. And the last bag will be five new, one old. That's twelve parts of each grain unequally divided among the bags. We need another bag or bin to hold the new mixture, a coffee can to measure, and let's go—"

"Brilliant," Stevie pronounced, and ripped open the first bag of old feed and began counting out five measures.

"Hold it," Carole said. "I just remembered something. We can't use the coffee can. We have to weigh the grain. Horses are fed by weight, not volume. All these bags weigh the same, but the bags with the new grain are larger. That would have been a bad mistake."

Lisa was surprised, but when she took another look at the sacks, she saw that Carole was absolutely right. She bent her head to her notebook. A few more scribbles, a few more cross-outs, some more calculations, and—

"Bingo!" Lisa announced. "Here's how many pounds of each we need in each bag."

Stevie hauled out a scale and the three of them got to

work. It was hard, but it wasn't unpleasant because they were working together. Carole weighed while Stevie mixed and Lisa kept track.

"Just think, Carole," Stevie said. "Lisa's going to spend an entire week without having to do one Pine Hollow chore!"

Lisa grinned at her friends. "Sounds too good to be true, doesn't it?" she asked, making a note of the next six pounds of mixture to be put in the sack they were working on. "Living on a tropical island, away from winter storms and grain that needs to be weighed . . ."

It sounded nice to Lisa even as she said it. She felt a quiver of excitement. She could almost feel the warm breeze and the hot sun on her back. She could almost smell the mangoes and the coconut oil. She could almost taste the fresh seafood and feel the soft sand beneath her feet, hear the sound of the azure waters lapping at the shore by her cabin. The picture seemed almost perfect. Still, something was missing and Lisa couldn't quite put her finger on it.

"Earth to Lisa!" Stevie said mischievously, startling Lisa out of her daydream. "There goes another six pounds," Stevie added as she stirred the feed vigorously.

Lisa checked her calculations. "That's all for that bag," she told the others.

"Keep mixing it, though," Carole said. "It's really important for the feed to be mixed thoroughly."

Stevie continued mixing. "Speaking of tropical islands," she said, "do you know why flamingos stand on one leg?"

"Unh-unh," Lisa said. It was actually something she'd never thought about. She didn't even know if there would be flamingos on San Marco. "Why?" she asked.

"Because if they picked up the other one, they'd fall down," Stevie replied, and grinned when Carole groaned.

It was then that Lisa realized the worst thing about her trip to San Marco. There would be no Stevie, and no Carole.

2

Lisa pressed her nose against the small window of the airplane. The water below was a stunning turquoise. Small boats dotted the surface. To the left, she could see an island. She wondered if that was San Marco. She felt the plane descend, and decided it was.

The island seemed to be ringed by white concave crescents.

"Beaches!" she said out loud. It was strange to think that within a very short time she could be on one.

Soon, the plane landed and Lisa followed her parents down the aisle and onto the tarmac. The hot, humid air of the tropical island hit her the instant she stepped out of the air-conditioned airplane.

"Oh," she said, surprised as she took her first breath of San Marco. The air was sweet with the scent of flowers, mixed in with the acrid smell of airplane fuel.

It took only a few minutes for the Atwoods to retrieve their luggage, pass through customs and immigration, and get into a taxi. Their hotel was a short drive from the airport. It seemed to Lisa that she'd barely gotten used to being on the ground when she found herself unpacking.

The contents of Lisa's suitcase, which had seemed so out of place in snowy, cold Virginia, were exactly right for San Marco. She had brought shorts and tank tops, bathing suits, T-shirts, a couple of cotton dresses, and her riding clothes. Not surprisingly, her riding clothes, with her boots and her hat, took up more than half of the space in her suitcase.

With a sigh of relief, Lisa took off her wool skirt and heavy sweater and replaced them with a bathing suit covered by a pair of turquoise shorts, a bright pink top, and a pair of sandals. She found her sunglasses, her sun hat, and her sunscreen.

"I'm ready for anything," she told her image in the mirror, and after checking with her parents and agreeing to meet them at the pool in an hour, she set out to explore.

The hotel, it turned out, was a long, narrow building, running parallel to the ocean. The dining room and public areas were situated in the center of the complex, close to the pool. Just beyond the pool, a perfect white beach stretched along the island's coast. The water was the same incredible blue she'd seen from the air. Even up close, the color was hard to believe.

Beaches and pools, however, were not what Lisa really wanted to find. She walked out to the other side of the hotel, which faced away from the beach, and looked for signs of the stable.

Before her arrival, Lisa had tried to imagine what a tropical island would be like. She had thought that it would be like Virginia in the summer, with palm trees. Now she knew that the idea came nowhere near the truth. It didn't take into account the heavy, humid air, the sweet scent—now minus airplane fuel—and the unusual trees and bushes. Even the grass felt different as it brushed her feet. It was coarser than the grass at home.

She glanced at the sky above her. It seemed impossible that this was the same sky she could see out her window in Willow Creek, but it was. Now it was clear, with a few scattered puffy white clouds. In the far distance, she could see a large mass of darker clouds.

Lisa followed a footpath through the hotel's garden and found herself at a dirt road. She looked for a sign or somebody to direct her, but no guide was in sight. Then she glanced at the road, and spotted the familiar marks of hooves. Feeling a little bit like Davy Crockett, she followed the hoofprints until they led her to her goal, the stable.

The stable was buzzing with activity. One group of riders had just returned from a trail ride, and another group was gathering to leave. Lisa was impressed with the horses. She could tell immediately that they were well cared for. The grooms waited attentively, holding the reins while the riders dismounted, and helping riders down.

A woman who was clearly in charge was standing in

the center of the yard giving the stablehands orders on which horses to put away and which to keep out. Lisa watched as the woman sized up the riders about to go on the trail, matching them with horses she thought they could manage.

"What do you mean, you've taken lessons?" she was asking a man.

"Well, I had some lessons a few years ago," the man answered vaguely.

"Walk, trot, and canter?" the instructor asked.

The man shrugged. "I guess so," he said.

"Ride Pal, then. He's the bay over there."

The man looked confused.

"Bay means brown with a black mane and tail," the instructor told him. "But, actually, I think you'll do better on Jasper, here." She patted the flank of a gray horse.

Lisa knew that the man's uncertainty about the three gaits and his unfamiliarity with horse colors had told the instructor a lot. As Lisa had learned, it was important to match riders and horses correctly or an instructor could have a disaster on her hands. Lisa thought the instructor had handled the situation well.

"You're not riding in *that* outfit!" the instructor said sharply. Lisa was surprised to find she was speaking to her.

"Oh, no," Lisa said. "I'm not riding today. We just got here and I'm looking around."

"Look all you want, but stay clear of the horses," the instructor said. "They're big animals."

The woman turned and began speaking to somebody

else as abruptly as she'd spoken to Lisa. Automatically, Lisa stepped back, out of the way. She entered the stable, hoping she wouldn't annoy anybody there.

Lisa liked the stable immediately. It was a white stucco building, unlike the wooden structures she was familiar with. It had a wide aisle and big stalls for each horse. Lisa counted twenty-eight stalls, plus a tack room and a feed room. About half the horses were outside, either leaving or coming back from the trail. The remaining horses stood patiently, munching at their hay and sipping at their water. One horse lifted his head curiously as Lisa walked by. Lisa paused. The horse stuck his head out over the door. Lisa patted him on his cheek and neck. He sniffed at her.

"I told you, they're big animals. Be careful!" the instructor said with annoyance. She'd entered the stable silently and now strode toward the tack room, carrying a broken stirrup leather in her hand.

"I'm okay," Lisa assured her, but she jumped back from the horse anyway, feeling very unwelcome. She was determined to ride, though.

"Can I ask you something?" she asked while the instructor rummaged through a rack of leathers.

"Not now," the woman said. "Wait until these riders are out, then I'll answer your questions. In the meantime, why don't you wait in the office?"

Lisa nodded and politely followed the woman's suggestion. She would much rather have waited in the stable, but it was clear the woman didn't trust her, and she wanted to get off on the right foot with the riding instructor.

Lisa sat on a rattan chair in the office and waited for the instructor to return. She suddenly felt very lonely and somehow out of place. She'd always felt as if she belonged at Pine Hollow once she'd made friends with Stevie and Carole. How could it be so different on San Marco? She realized with some dismay that she'd only been out of Willow Creek for about six hours and she was already homesick. *More like stablesick*, she told herself, and smiled at her own joke. It made her feel a little better.

After a few minutes, the riders dispersed, some on foot, headed for the pool, others on horseback, going out on the trail. The instructor entered the office.

"Well, what can I do for you?" she asked.

"I want to sign up for a ride," Lisa began.

The woman, whose nametag introduced her as Frederica, just half grunted in acknowledgment.

"I've been taking lessons for about six months," Lisa continued. "I can walk, trot, canter, and have begun jumping."

"Six months? Then we'll put you on the beginner trail ride tomorrow at eight-thirty," Frederica said.

"I'm an intermediate," Lisa said a little impatiently. She was surprised to hear herself contradict Frederica. It really wasn't like her to stand up to an adult, but she knew that if she got into the beginners' group, she'd never go faster than a walk.

Frederica frowned. "You've only been riding six months—"

"But I ride a lot—twice a week. And I went to riding camp. I'm in a Pony Club."

Frederica shrugged. "Okay, I'll let you try the intermediate ride. That's at ten o'clock. Here, fill this out. Get your parents' signatures, too."

She handed Lisa a registration card and then abruptly left the office.

Lisa glanced at the card, decided to fill it out later, stuck it in her pocket, and left the office. She had the feeling that a swim in the pool would feel really good about now. At least, it was certain to feel better than sitting in the office at the stable, trying to convince Frederica that she actually knew which end of the horse went first!

As Lisa walked back along the roadway, she spotted the first genuinely friendly face she'd seen since she'd arrived at the stable.

"Hi, my name's Jill. Are you a rider, too?" the girl asked. She looked about eleven years old, a little younger than Lisa. She had bright red curly hair and a cluster of freckles sprinkled across her nose and cheeks.

"I'm Lisa," she replied. "And yes, I am a rider. I'm going on the intermediate ride tomorrow at ten. What about you?"

"Me, too. Great," Jill said. "Are you pretty good?"

Lisa thought for a second. If Jill had asked her that question an hour ago, she wouldn't have hesitated to say yes, but now, Frederica's doubt seemed to have affected her.

"I don't know," she said. "I've only been riding less than a year, but I do ride a lot."

"Like once a week?" Jill asked.

"No, more like twice a week, and then there's my Pony Club. But when I was at camp last summer, I guess I rode about every day. I'm learning to jump, too."

"Wow! You really know your stuff, don't you?" Jill said, clearly impressed. "You're just going to love this ride. Tomorrow will be my third time. Frederica leads it. She's really strict, but it's great and you won't have any trouble at all."

Somehow, Jill's confidence was infectious. *I do really know my stuff,* Lisa thought. She knew how to ride. Equally important, she knew how to take care of horses. She knew how to feed them, groom them, even how to take care of them when they were sick. She was good. She'd learned a lot in six months. It didn't matter what Frederica thought. She'd show that woman how good she really was!

The two girls walked back toward the hotel and fell into an easy conversation about horses. Jill lived near Boston, and she had a neighbor with a horse she could ride occasionally. She told Lisa how much she loved horses and riding and they compared experiences. Lisa was a little pleased to find that she'd had more instruction than Jill. Jill had learned a lot from her friend, but Lisa had been studying harder.

"You mean you actually take *tests* about horse care in your Pony Club?" Jill asked.

"Oh, sure," Lisa said. "And they're not easy, either." Lisa told her about all the skills they had to study and practice and how hard Max made them work, both in the Pony Club, Horse Wise, and in riding. Jill had obviously never come across anything like it. She was extremely impressed. And as far as Lisa was concerned, Jill's admiration went a long way toward making up for the hard time she'd had convincing Frederica that she knew what she was doing.

They arrived at the lobby of the resort and agreed to meet by the pool in ten minutes. As she headed for her room to get her beach towel, Lisa reflected that she was glad she'd met Jill, although it wasn't exactly the same as having Stevie and Carole there. But Jill seemed nice enough and she was interested in horses. That had been enough for a start with Stevie and Carole. Lisa hoped it would be with Jill, too.

LISA FELT A little out of place the next morning at breakfast. Almost everybody, including her own parents, was wearing shorts or a bathing suit. She would be in a bathing suit by noon, but for now, she was wearing breeches and boots and carrying a hard hat because she was going riding.

"Good morning, Lisa!" Jill greeted her cheerfully, pulling out the chair next to hers at the breakfast table. Lisa was relieved to see that Jill was dressed the same way she was. She relaxed right away.

"Good morning," Lisa said, and smiled at her new friend.

"Hi there, Mr. and Mrs. A.," Jill said. Lisa winced and tried not to look at her parents. Jill had only met them very briefly the day before. The Atwoods were rather formal people, and after that greeting Lisa was certain they wouldn't approve of Jill.

But both of her parents were unfazed. "Good morning, Jill, how's it going?" Mr. Atwood asked warmly. "Looking forward to your ride?" Lisa remembered then that her parents could occasionally surprise her.

"Oh, yes!" Jill said. "And Lisa's just going to love it, too. She'll see a whole part of this island you can't see at all from the resort. It's something special! And because Lisa's such a good rider, I just know we'll have a great time. Yesterday, before you guys got here, there was a total amateur on the ride. We had to stop all the time so Frederica could explain things he really should have known. It was so boring. I hope it'll be better today. It's got to be better, though, because Lisa will be there!"

Lisa gulped down the rest of her breakfast. That didn't please her mother, but at least Mrs. Atwood didn't say anything.

"Let's go." Lisa pushed her chair back, picked up her hat, and headed for the door. Jill followed.

The stable was a five-minute walk from the main building. As they walked, Jill continued to tell Lisa about the route they would take on their ride and how much Lisa was going to love it. Lisa was already convinced, but she didn't mind the extra sales pitch. Jill was no Carole or Stevie, but she was okay. Besides, Jill was there, and Carole and Stevie weren't.

Like the day before, the stable area was a flurry of organized confusion. Frederica stood on the mounting block, directing stablehands and riders like a conductor with an orchestra.

"Mr. Hellman, you ride Pal. He's the bay over by the fence. Alain, help Mr. Hellman, please." Stablehands adjusted stirrups and held bridles for the riders while Frederica oversaw everything.

"Ah, yes, Lisa," Frederica said thoughtfully when Lisa approached her. "The new rider. You take Velvet. That's the gray mare under the palm tree. Jill, you're on Tiger again. He's next to Velvet. Alain, help these girls as soon as Mr. Hellman is in the saddle."

Lisa didn't need any help. She could adjust her own stirrups and mount a horse without a stablehand to help her. She wanted to show Frederica that, as well. Confidently, she approached Velvet, who waited patiently in the shade of a tall palm tree.

Velvet regarded her curiously, flicking her ears like antennae. Lisa liked that. It was usually a sign that the horse was alert and responsive. She patted Velvet's neck, admiring the mare's smooth coat. She scratched the horse's forehead and rubbed her cheek. After that, Velvet's curiosity was apparently satisfied, for she turned her attention to the sparse grass that grew at the foot of the tree. Lisa turned hers to the horse's tack.

First, Lisa checked the girth and found she had to tighten it a notch. Velvet stood quietly while she did. Lisa then adjusted her stirrups and was mounting the horse when Alain arrived to help her. She told him she was fine and that he should help Jill. Lisa could tell that

Jill was impressed with her confidence. She felt grateful to Max for insisting that all his riders learn to do these things for themselves.

"Ready?" Frederica asked a few minutes later. Lisa was. So was everybody else. Frederica explained the familiar ground rules of a trail ride—"Stay in a single line, evenly spaced, following my lead"—and it was time to start.

There were seven trail riders, not including Frederica. Frederica had arranged the line so that Lisa was third and Jill was fifth. Lisa wished they could have been together, but Frederica was definite about the way she wanted things done. Lisa and Jill followed her request without comment.

They walked their horses out of the stable area, past a schooling ring with low jumps, and followed a well-worn trail through the hotel's gardens. Soon, they were on open grass, headed toward the ocean.

It was a magnificent sight. In the first place, it was a glorious day. The sky was a deep, rich blue with only a few wisps of clouds. The grassy area they were on led to a narrow grove of palms that edged the beach. The beach itself was a white crescent of sand, meeting the turquoise waters of the Caribbean. Lisa blinked her eyes to make sure the water's color was real. But the color didn't change. It remained the same startling blue it had been when she had first seen it.

"Prepare to trot!" Frederica called from the front of the line.

Without any signal from Lisa, Velvet began trotting. It always concerned Lisa when the horse she was riding changed gaits without instructions from her. It meant Velvet was paying more attention to the horse in front of her than she was to Lisa. It meant Lisa wasn't in control. The jolt she felt when Velvet began trotting proved it, and proved something else. The mare had definitely gotten her name from the softness of her coat and not the smoothness of her gait! Velvet's trot was short and jerky, catching Lisa by surprise. It took a few seconds for Lisa to recover and begin posting, but once she did, she was fine. The only complaint she had, in fact, was that at a trot, the scenery went by too quickly.

The horses sped through the coconut grove toward the beach. As they approached the sand, Frederica slowed her horse down to a walk. All the others riders followed suit. Velvet's shift in gaits was just as jerky as her trot. Lisa was jolted forward with the sudden slowing down. She got her balance again and settled back into the saddle.

The beach was filling up with sunbathers from their hotel. Lisa looked for her parents and was relieved when she didn't see them. No matter how good Lisa was, it always made her mother nervous to see her on horseback. At that moment, since she wasn't feeling very confident with Velvet, the last thing Lisa wanted to think about was how her mother would feel if she saw her!

Soon, the horses were past the part of the beach where there were swimmers. Frederica rose and turned around in her saddle. She lifted her hand as a signal to all the riders.

"Prepare to canter!" she called.

Lisa was glad they wouldn't be trotting again right away. It was her experience that horses with rough trots usually had very smooth canters. She was looking forward to the gentle rocking of the three-beat gait.

She held the reins tight and kept her legs on Velvet. It was a way of reminding the mare who was in charge. After the horse in front of her began cantering, Lisa moved her right foot behind Velvet's girth and touched her belly. Velvet responded instantly, lurching into a canter that was just as jerky and rough as her trot.

Lisa gripped the mare tightly with her legs. She sat as deeply in the saddle as she could and she kept her hands still. Within a few seconds, she had her balance back and could feel the regular, though rough, rhythm of the horse's canter.

Riding Velvet was hard work. The one thing going for Lisa was that their path was clear and relatively straight. They were following the gentle curve of the beach, and the ground was hard and smooth. It took all of Lisa's concentration to hold firmly with her legs and sit deeply in the saddle through Velvet's jerky canter. She sighed audibly when Frederica's hand went up, a signal to return to the walk.

Automatically, Lisa leaned forward and patted Velvet's neck in appreciation. The horse may have had an awkward and uncomfortable gait, but she had done what Lisa had asked.

The group walked for a while, and Lisa had time to admire the scenery. The horses trailed along the beach and then crossed a runoff ditch, taking them into water several feet deep and about twenty feet wide. Lisa was very glad for the waterproof riding boots Stevie had given her as a Christmas present. Velvet seemed to enjoy sloshing through the gentle surf at the edge of the sea.

"Prepare to canter!" Frederica called out again when the riders were all clear of the water. Lisa didn't like the feeling of dread that clutched at her stomach at those words. She wasn't used to it when it came to riding, but the feeling was unmistakable. She gripped Velvet as well as she could with her legs and then, when the time came, signaled for a canter.

At first, things went fine. Velvet paid more attention to Lisa than to the horse in front of her. The problem came when Lisa began paying more attention to Velvet than to the trail. The trail swung into the wooded area to the left, toward a hill. Velvet swung with it, but Lisa didn't. She just wasn't prepared for the turn and flew right out of the saddle, landing with an undignified thump on the soft earth at the edge of the beach.

"Aargh!" she grunted, rolling out of the way of oncoming horses. Fortunately, she had fallen off the path so she wasn't in danger. Once Velvet was free of her rider, she halted, bringing the rest of the riders to a halt as well. Before Lisa could even stand, Frederica was off her horse and by her side.

"Don't move," Frederica instructed her.

"I'm fine," Lisa said. "I just lost my balance on the turn. It shouldn't have happened. The ground is soft here. I'm really okay."

Frederica told her to wait anyway. Sometimes a rider

can be seriously hurt without knowing it. Lisa knew it always paid to wait a few seconds to make sure everything was in working order before standing up.

Frederica offered her a hand, but Lisa stood up on her own. "See? I'm really fine," she assured Frederica and the other riders. They all seemed relieved. Lisa took Velvet's reins from Jill, who had held them for her. She remounted, checked her tack, patted Velvet reassuringly, and nodded.

"I'm ready. Let's go," she said. One of the first things Lisa had ever learned about horseback riding was that it is important for the rider to get back in the saddle and ride again after a fall. Falls happen, and the best way for a rider to restore confidence is to prove to herself that one fall isn't the end of a riding career.

Lisa promised herself that she'd be a little more careful in the future. Paying attention to her horse was important, but so was paying attention to the trail. She was a better rider than that, and she knew it. *One fall doesn't mean anything,* she told herself.

"Don't worry," Jill said from behind her. "It could happen to anybody."

Of course it could, Lisa thought. *Couldn't it?*

Dear Stevie and Carole,

It is so beautiful here, you wouldn't believe it. The Caribbean looks like somebody painted it this gorgeous blue color.

Now to important stuff. I was on a trail ride this morning. Again, incredible scenery (see the picture on

the other side). We rode on the beach and into the surf!
(Stevie—love those boots you gave me.) Rode through
palm groves, too. Can't wait to do it again tomorrow.
Wish you were here.

Love,
Lisa

4

STEVIE WAS BRUSHING her teeth, but she was barely aware of it. She was deep in a daydream. It was pretty much the same one she'd been having for weeks, ever since Phil had invited her to the New Year's dance. While she brushed her teeth with her right hand, she swept her hair up to the top of her head with her left arm, imagining the tumble of curls that would be held by a spray of pink tea roses. The dream also involved yards and yards of blue chiffon that seemed to float with her across the dance floor. Phil looked deeply into her eyes. She blinked seductively—

Wait a minute, she told herself, coming to earth. She couldn't blink seductively unless she was wearing mascara. She'd have to buy some, and she needed money for that.

Quickly, she finished brushing her teeth, rinsed out,

ran a comb through her hair, and dashed downstairs before her mother left for her office.

"Mom!" she called out, halting her mother at the kitchen door. "I'm going to need some mascara. Can you leave me a couple of dollars—"

"Allowance gone already?" Mrs. Lake asked, leaning heavily on the final word. It didn't bode well for Stevie.

"Well, I just had to get some cologne, see, because, well, I've got to have that, and I know I'll want mascara—probably deep blue to accent the dress—"

"What dress?" Mrs. Lake asked.

It didn't bode well at all for Stevie.

"You know, the one we're going to get for the dance?" she said meekly.

"*We?*" her mother countered.

The battle was lost—at least for the day. Her mother was making it very clear that she wasn't going to give Stevie any more money and, if Stevie read the signals correctly, it was even looking dubious that she'd be able to get a dress. It was time to retreat.

"Hey, no problem, Mom. I don't want to make you late for work. I don't need any money just now, anyway. I'm really fine. You go ahead. Have fun at the office, okay?"

Stevie's mother said something as she passed through the door, but Stevie wasn't sure what it was. It sounded a lot like "Hmmmph."

Stevie wasn't too worried. She'd find a way to convince her mother to get her a dress *and* some mascara. She always found a way to do things she wanted and she wanted very much to have a perfect dress for this dance, as well as mascara to make her eyelashes seductive. In the meantime, however, she wanted to discuss the whole situation with somebody who would understand. Who better than one of her best friends? She reached for the phone and dialed Carole's number.

The phone rang six times. There was no answer. Stevie let it ring some more. It was only eight-thirty in the morning on a school vacation day. Where on earth could Carole be? Finally, after sixteen rings, Stevie gave up.

She poured herself a bowl of cereal, then poured half of it back into the box. Stevie was very diet-conscious these days, since she was looking for The Perfect Dress and it would be awful if she found it and it didn't fit her. She pondered while she ate the cereal without sugar.

By the third tasteless mouthful, Stevie decided that even horses couldn't eat this stuff without sugar, and that even if she couldn't buy a dress yet, she could certainly look for one. Then, when she had The Perfect Dress, it would be much easier to convince her mother to buy it.

She threw out the rest of the cereal, rinsed the dish and put it in the dishwasher, and went up to her room to get dressed. It only took two phone calls to find somebody to drive her to the mall. She was in business.

CAROLE WAS ALREADY at Pine Hollow. She didn't want to miss a minute of time that she could spend with Starlight for the remainder of her winter vacation. After all, she wouldn't have this much time for him again until summer.

Starlight was a young horse. He would become six on January first. Most riding horses began their serious training at about four and were pretty well trained by the time they were seven or eight. Starlight was obviously an apt pupil, but he was a bit unschooled and Carole wanted to work with him as often as possible.

She tightened his girth as much as she could and then, when he let his breath out, she slipped it one hole tighter on the buckle.

"Can't fool me, Starlight," she teased. The horse blinked his eyes, but it looked as if he'd winked. Carole was sure he understood.

Laughing to herself, she took hold of his reins and led him though the stable, through the outdoor schooling ring, and into a small paddock, which abutted the ring. She didn't need much space for what she was working on today, which was mounting and dismounting.

Carole had noticed that Starlight had the bad habit of stepping forward when she tried to mount him. She knew that as a rider, she had two choices. She could let him keep his bad manners and learn to mount a moving horse, or she could teach him better. She decided on the second option.

"Whoa, there, Starlight," she said, drawing him to a halt. She gathered the reins in her left hand, and, holding them taut but not too tight, rested that hand on his withers and aimed her left foot for the stirrup.

Starlight recognized the signs instantly and began stepping forward.

"Hooo!" Carole said sharply, tightening the reins. He

34

stopped. She kept pressure on the reins until he stepped back to where she had begun mounting him.

She began the process again, and again Starlight misbehaved. She repeated the lesson a third time. This time, Starlight stepped forward only two steps before stopping, and returned very quickly. He was making progress, but Carole didn't reward him with a pat. He wouldn't get that until he did it right.

The fourth time, Carole could feel him shift his weight as if he were about to step forward, but then he stopped moving altogether, allowing her to mount him. In an instant, she was in the saddle. She leaned forward and patted him briskly on his neck.

"Atta boy," she said, giving him a loose rein while she patted him. A loose rein was a reward that signaled him that what he was doing at that time was just right. He had stood still while she mounted him, and that was what Carole had asked him to do.

Having taught him that much, she had him walk around the little paddock and then let him trot. He changed gaits smoothly and willingly. Carole was thankful she didn't have to work with him on that. She then drew him to a halt and swung her right leg over his rump to dismount. Starlight apparently didn't realize that dismounting required the same motionless patience that mounting did. He stepped backward this time.

Carole immediately brought her right leg back over and into its stirrup, tightening the rein and talking sharply to the horse at the same time. He stopped moving and stepped forward at her command, returning to the place she wanted to dismount. It took five tries before he would stand still for her dismount. Eventually, though, he behaved.

But when it came time to remount, Starlight was back to his old tricks. Carole knew that that was just the way it was in training a horse. The animal needed to be taught things time and time again until its good behavior was completely automatic.

Carole worked with Starlight for two hours, mounting and dismounting until she could feel tenderness in her own thighs and shoulders from all the exercise. By the time the session was over, she was sure Starlight had learned something. She just hoped he would remember some of it the next time she took him out.

By then Starlight was as tired as she was. She led him back to his stall, removed his tack, groomed him, and fed him before heading for the bus to take her home.

Carole was tired, but not too tired to talk to Stevie. She really wanted to call her and tell her about all the work she and Starlight had done that day.

When she got home, she flopped into the big over-stuffed armchair in her living room, reached for the phone, and dialed Stevie's number.

Stevie's brother Chad picked the phone up on the second ring. He told Carole that Stevie wasn't there and he didn't have any idea where she was. Furthermore, he didn't know when she'd be home, and asked Carole to please hang up the phone because he was expecting an important call.

Carole was so tired she wasn't really annoyed, but she was disappointed.

"CAN I HELP you?" a saleswoman asked Stevie. At that moment, Stevie was looking at a chiffon dress. There were two things wrong with it. First of all, it was green, not the blue she'd dreamed about, and second of all, if she read the price tag correctly—and it was hard to believe—it would cost her approximately four years' worth of allowance.

"Can I help you?" the woman repeated her question pointedly. Stevie had the feeling that the saleswoman didn't trust her.

"Uh, well," Stevie began, "maybe. Does this dress come in blue?" she asked.

"No," the woman said. That was all she said, too. She didn't offer to show Stevie something else in blue. Stevie suspected the only thing she actually wanted to show her was the door.

"Well, I really wanted this in blue," Stevie said. "It would go so well with the interior of my limousine."

Stevie turned on her heel and walked out, hoping she'd made the woman feel bad about letting a big sale slip through her fingers.

This was the fifth store Stevie had tried at the mall. So far, the only thing she'd found that she might actually have a chance of talking her mother into buying for her was a navy blue mascara on sale for $1.49. The dresses were all out of her price range, or just plain ugly.

Shopping had never been Stevie's favorite activity and this trip was no exception. She wished she had a friend there to help her. *Lisa would know what to do,* Stevie thought wistfully. Mrs. Atwood even worked at the mall part-time and would know where all the best dresses were to be found—on sale. But both Lisa and Mrs. Atwood were on the tropical island of San Marco.

5

"So, do you hurt anyplace this morning?" Jill asked as she caught up with Lisa on her way to her next trail ride the following morning.

Lisa didn't have any idea what Jill was talking about. "Hurt?" she asked.

"You know. From the fall you took yesterday."

"Oh, that. No, of course not," Lisa answered, but it wasn't exactly the truth. She had a big bruise where she sat down. As long as she wasn't sitting, she didn't think about it, and even when she was sitting, she didn't think about how she'd gotten it. "I'm fine," Lisa assured Jill.

"Good, because I'm sure Frederica will want you to take it easy today after a fall like that, but if you're okay . . ."

Jill let her words hang in the air in a way that told Lisa Jill did not believe she was okay.

"Look," Lisa said. "I got distracted and lost my balance and fell off my horse. It shouldn't have happened. I know better, but it happened and I'm fine, okay?"

"Sure, Lisa," Jill said. There it was again. It was an unmistakable say-what-you-want-but-I-don't-believe-you tone.

Lisa decided to change the subject. "I remember the first trail ride I ever took," she began. She told Jill about the first time she'd gone out into the fields around Pine Hollow with Stevie and Carole. Stevie had gotten confused about which fields were occupied and which they could cross. The girls had found themselves being chased away from a gate by a very angry bull, and Lisa had followed her friends, jumping over a four-foot-high fence! The memory of that jump helped to remind Lisa that she really was a pretty good rider.

"Sure, Lisa," Jill said again.

The two girls walked in silence for the next few minutes. Lisa didn't like the way Jill was making her feel, but she decided to ignore it and enjoy the spectacular scenery instead. The path to the stable was lined with brightly colored exotic blossoms that she had seen sold in flower shops at home for outrageous prices. Lisa breathed in the delicious sweetness, letting it calm and restore her.

"Good morning, Frederica," Jill said cheerfully, greeting the instructor, who was waiting for the return of another group of riders.

"Good morning, Jill, and—uh—Lisa. Are you riding with us again today?"

"Of course!" Lisa said. "The trail is beautiful and I don't want to miss a chance to ride."

"Of course not," Frederica said. "But there is another trail you could take at the one o'clock ride. It's a little less challenging and—"

Lisa could hardly believe her ears. Less challenging? The one o'clock ride was probably a beginners' ride! That meant only walking, no trotting, no cantering. Beginners' rides had their place, but only for beginners, not experienced riders like herself.

"No, Frederica," she said firmly. "I'd really prefer to take this ride. I can do it and I'm sure you'll understand, I need to do it."

Frederica looked at her for a few seconds before agreeing. "I do understand, Lisa. It's okay. Ride Jasper, will you?"

Lisa recalled that Jasper was the horse Frederica had assigned to the man who didn't know what color a bay horse was. Jasper was obviously the horse Frederica gave to people who belonged on beginners' rides. Lisa was beginning to feel very annoyed about the whole situation. The fact was that she was a good rider. She'd lost her balance and taken a tumble off a horse with a jerky gait. So what? A lot of people fell off horses. It didn't mean they weren't good riders. Now, here it had happened to her and all of a sudden Jill and Frederica seemed to have the impression that she didn't know one thing about riding. That wasn't fair, but even more important, it wasn't true.

Lisa hid her disappointment and walked over to Jasper. He greeted her with a look of indifference. Lisa felt the same way.

She checked his girth, adjusted his stirrups, mounted, and was ready to go in a matter of minutes.

"Let me check your girth," Alain said.

"I did it already, but you can check again," Lisa said shortly. Alain did check it again. He also checked her stirrups.

"Very good!" he said, complimenting her work.

"Thanks." Lisa didn't think it was much of a compliment. Any Pine Hollow rider could do those things.

"Riders up! Let's go!" Frederica called, lining them up in the order she wanted. Lisa was dismayed to see that she was the second-to-last person in the line, and the rider behind her was Jill. That meant that Frederica thought that she was at risk of being thrown again and didn't want a lot of riders behind her who might endanger her. Worst of all, it meant that Frederica considered Jill to be a better rider than she was. Lisa was humiliated.

It didn't help, either, when Jill started giving her little tips about riding as they rode.

"If you watch where you're going, it will make it easier to steer the horse," Jill suggested. A little later, she said, "Once your horse has gotten to the gait and speed you want, you should loosen up on the reins just to let him know what he's doing is right. And we're going to turn to the right up here. Move your right hand out and put pressure on with your left leg."

This was all stuff from Lisa's first lessons. She knew it

all by heart and didn't need a refresher course, especially not from someone two years younger than she was. Lisa was irritated by Jill, but she was even more irritated by the idea that Frederica had probably put Jill up to it!

There was only one solution: ignore it. Lisa shut her ears to the flow of helpful suggestions coming from behind her and concentrated on her ride.

The group followed the same path they had ridden the day before and, once again, it was breathtakingly beautiful. The group trotted briskly through the palm grove toward the beach and then walked to cool the horses before trotting along the edge of the water. Lisa's parents were on the beach, and waved cheerfully as Lisa rode by. Lisa put both reins in one hand and returned their wave.

"You should always keep both hands on the reins," Jill reminded her. "That way you keep even pressure on the horse's mouth."

It was all Lisa could do to keep from snapping back that in Western riding it was customary to use one hand and she was almost as good at Western riding as she was at English. But Lisa had the suspicion that that wouldn't impress Jill much.

Lisa sensed her own apprehension as they approached the place where she'd fallen off the day before. She gripped Jasper tightly with her legs, not so much to signal the horse as to hold on tighter. Jasper responded by moving forward faster. Lisa was prepared. She took the curve easily and smoothly and sighed with relief when they had passed it.

"Good!" Jill said from behind. Lisa didn't bother to answer.

The trail then wound up a hill to a grassy promontory that overlooked the Caribbean. Frederica paused at the top, allowing all the riders to gaze at the gorgeous scenery. Oddly, Lisa noticed that Jill pulled her horse back away from the group while they gazed at the ocean. Lisa thought Jill seemed genuinely uncomfortable with the height and the sheer drop to the ocean. *Too bad,* Lisa thought, taking a final glance. The sight was truly spectacular.

The walk back down the hill was tricky, and abruptly brought Lisa's attention to her own difficulties. When Jasper broke into a trot coming off the hill, she slowed him and controlled him as he regained his place in line.

They entered another palm grove then. Lisa saw that there was a small, shabby house in the grove with enclosed yards around it. One little yard held a family of goats. Another had a chicken coop. A little boy stood outside the coop and tossed grain for the hens to eat. But the child never took his eyes off the riders who passed his home. The look on his face was intensely curious. Lisa found herself wondering how different that child's life was from her own very comfortable one in Virginia. She thought perhaps she had as much to learn from this little boy as he did from her. She also thought it would be unlikely that either would get the opportunity to do that learning.

"Prepare to canter!" Frederica called from the front of

the line. Lisa felt a tightening in her stomach and recognized her own fear. She didn't like the feeling at all.

She gripped the horse tightly with her legs, shortened her reins, sat deeply in the saddle, and signaled Jasper to canter. He did. Jasper's canter was much smoother than Velvet's. It was almost a lumbering gait, as though the horse had to labor to maintain it. Lisa gave him a little bit more rein and kept her legs tight against his belly.

They followed the trail through the palm grove. Lisa kept her eyes forward so she wouldn't be fooled by a curve as she had been on Velvet. It definitely helped her riding. It also allowed her to see a family of eight piglets scurry across the bridle path. Lisa thought they were probably headed for the house and the little boy, who might feed them. At last the riders came clear of the palm grove and rode down a gentle slope into a marsh, still cantering. Frederica then led them right into the water. The horses sloshed willingly through the swamp, but Lisa wasn't prepared for the change of speed the water caused. As soon as Jasper's hooves began slogging through the mud, he slowed. Lisa didn't.

It didn't matter how tightly she gripped him, the sudden change of speed was more than she could handle. She flew right over Jasper's neck and landed in the mud. This time, she couldn't roll and evade her own oncoming horse fast enough. Jasper shied to the left, but not fast enough to keep from kicking her in the knee. Jill yanked on her horse's reins, but he too ran into Lisa.

In an instant, Frederica was by her side.

"Don't move," she instructed Lisa once again.

This time, Lisa obeyed. She hurt. She didn't want to move.

"Where do you hurt?" Frederica asked.

Lisa told her about the bang on her knee and on her shoulder, where Jill's horse had struck her.

Frederica asked Lisa to move her leg and then her knee. When Lisa did so without difficulty, Frederica helped her stand up. Another rider brought Jasper back to Lisa.

"Can you ride again?" Frederica asked.

Lisa was surprised to find herself hesitating before she answered. "Yes," she said finally.

With help, she got back into the saddle, feeling yesterday's bruise in her seat along with her two new ones. She also felt the soggy filth of the marsh water she'd tumbled into. Some of it even sloshed around inside her waterproof boot.

The rest of the ride went by in a haze. About the only thing Lisa noticed was that Jill had stopped giving her riding tips. Lisa decided that meant Jill had probably given up on her as a hopeless case. She didn't care. All she wanted to do was to finish out the ride and get to her room.

The riders finally reached the stable. Lisa rode Jasper over to a shady spot away from the other riders, hoping they would take the hint and leave her alone. It didn't work. One by one, every rider except Jill came up to her and told her how sorry they were that she'd fallen off and how they hoped she didn't hurt too much.

They had no idea how much she hurt, but it wasn't the bruises that hurt the most. It was her confidence.

Lisa shook her head in amazement. For the last six months, she had always thought of herself as a rider, a good rider. She took lessons, she belonged to a Pony Club, she'd even been to riding camp. She and her friends had won a gymkhana. They'd even competed in a rodeo and won a prize there. She had always been a good rider, but how could something that was so right at home be so wrong on the beautiful tropical island of San Marco?

As quickly as she could, Lisa left the stable and headed back to her room to change. Almost everybody she passed on the way saw her muddy clothes, and the looks on their faces told her that they all knew exactly what had happened to her. That mystified Lisa. How could all those strangers know when she herself had no idea what had really happened?

All she knew was that she wasn't a rider anymore and maybe never would be again.

6

LISA DIDN'T GO riding the next day. The hotel operator woke her up bright and early at her parents' request so she could get ready to begin a tour of the whole island of San Marco. The trip, including a beach picnic, would take all day. Her parents said they hoped Lisa wasn't too disappointed that she wouldn't be able to ride. Lisa assured them she wasn't. In fact, though she didn't tell them, she was actually relieved.

Right after breakfast, she and her parents met their driver, Ben, a cheerful large man with a large van to accommodate them and their picnic. Lisa's father had spent some time the evening before looking at local maps to decide exactly what sights they wanted to see. Ben took a look at the list, crumpled it, stuffed it in his pocket, and said, "No, no, I show you the island—my island."

Since he said it so nicely, there seemed to be nothing to do but to agree.

Ben opened doors for Lisa and her mother and saw to it that everybody was comfortable in the seats. He secured the picnic basket in the back and then climbed into the van himself. "First, the rain forest," he announced, slamming his own door to add emphasis to his intentions.

"Sounds good to me," Mr. Atwood said, fastening his seat belt.

San Marco was a volcanic island, and that meant that among other things, it was very mountainous. The roads followed the irregular terrain, carved into the mountainsides. On one side, dense forest covered land that seemed to rise straight up from the road. On the other side, a sheer cliff led to the sea below. Sometimes the road was so narrow that Lisa felt they were going to drive off it any minute and had to close her eyes. When she opened them, she noticed that her mother was doing the same thing. Her father chatted amiably with Ben, who followed the rutted and curvy road up and down mountains.

There was one mountain that seemed to be in the middle of a cloud at the end of a rainbow. "Look at that!" Lisa said, pointing to it.

"That's the rain forest," Ben explained. "It's usually raining in there, so there is usually a rainbow pointing the way to it."

Within a few minutes, Ben had pulled into a small parking lot in the rain forest. They got out of the van to explore.

The forest was a small area, clearly defined from a distance by the cloud and the rainbow, and it was a place unlike any that Lisa had ever seen.

The vegetation was lush, with thick ground cover, palmlike ferns, middle-height trees, and tall trees that seemed like an umbrella, shading the whole area. The air was rich and humid, filled with the sweet smells of tropical flowers, which Lisa was becoming used to, but also filled with the lush smell of the fertile forest.

Ben showed them where fruit trees grew in the wild. He picked up a ripe lime from the ground and gave it to Lisa. He pointed out the orchids. He wasn't going to take one until he spotted one with a broken stem that would be withering soon. Carefully, he broke the stem the rest of the way and put the flower behind Mrs. Atwood's ear.

"You look very exotic!" Lisa told her mother, who grinned.

"Many things grow here that grow nowhere else," Ben said, indicating all the lush greenery that surrounded them. "Our rain forest is precious to us for its gifts and we take care of it in return." He pointed to the signs prohibiting visitors from taking anything from the plants.

Lisa had studied rain forests in school. She remembered how valuable they were as homes for thousands of animals and insects, how they alone provided a growing environment for many, many kinds of plants, and how they were being destroyed throughout the world. Now, standing there on a craggy mountain on a small volcanic island, she understood for the first time what the loss would mean to the world if people continued to destroy rain forests.

"And here is our rain forest botanical garden," Ben said, showing the Atwoods a path that led up a gentle slope. They all followed the path, reading the signs in front of each tree and bush. It seemed to Lisa that every houseplant or exotic flower she'd ever known grew wild in the rain forest of San Marco.

"This looks like our living room!" she teased her mother, who collected exotic plants.

"How right you are, and how beautiful they are. Look at that!" Mrs. Atwood pointed to a large bush with startling red leaves. It was a poinsettia, but it didn't look anything like the little ones they had at Christmas in their house. It was almost a tree and it was stunning.

At the end of the path, the Atwoods found themselves looking at a fifteen-foot-high waterfall that plunged into a pool that fed a stream that no doubt helped to keep all the plants green.

Lisa thought she could have watched the water come over the ridge of rocks all day long. Ben had something else in mind.

"Now the volcano," he announced, shooing them toward his van.

The volcano was only a few miles away, but it took them a long time to drive to it along the rutted roads. There was a hand-painted sign indicating the turnoff to the volcano, but Lisa wouldn't have needed to see a sign; she could smell its sulfurous fumes from a half mile away.

"This is an inactive volcano, but there is still activity there," Ben said, thinking he had explained something. The confused looks on the Atwoods' faces must have told him differently. "I mean, it is not going to erupt again, but there are hot springs bubbling all the time. Come, I show you."

The Atwoods got out of the van and followed Ben. He introduced them to some friends of his who worked at the volcano. They all walked across the rocky terrain, toward the sulfur pools. Ben pointed out a puddle on the ground and told Lisa to feel the water. It was warm. Another puddle was situated closer to the bubbling pools. Lisa felt that, too. It was hotter than the first. The next puddle was hotter still, and the one that followed was bubbling. Lisa didn't touch it.

When they could see into what had once been the crater of the volcano, they noticed several different bubbling pools, all filled with dank, opaque water, and all smelling fiercely of sulfur. It was hard to imagine what they were like on the inside, but Lisa wasn't tempted to find out, especially when Ben told her that the liquid had been measured at 350 degrees Fahrenheit!

They walked around the mouth of the crater and found rocks containing sulfur and iron, which Lisa planned to take back to her class. As she carefully pocketed the stones, Ben announced it was time for their next stop.

"Now we go to the market!"

He drove them into a small town. The entire center of the town was taken up with an open-air market where townspeople bought, sold, and traded their wares.

Lisa and her mother found some wonderful hats and baskets they wanted to buy. Mr. Atwood bought a shirt and a sunhat. He also bought a leather wallet for Ben, who had been admiring it at one of the shops. Lisa was glad they got him a present. He was showing them wonderful things and giving them a lovely time.

Ben proudly tucked his money into his new wallet and then announced their next activity.

"Picnic time!"

They all piled into his van and he drove them to the ocean. Ben explained that there were two kinds of beaches on the island—Caribbean and Atlantic. The beach near their hotel was Caribbean. Now they would see what the Atlantic was like.

At first, Lisa didn't think it was very different. The whole island was surrounded with the same bright turquoise water. They spread out their blanket and picnic on an empty beach just off the main road. Then they all stripped down to their bathing suits and headed for the water.

The Atlantic water *was* different. It was a little bit cooler and the surf was higher. Maybe that had more to do with the angle of the beach than the source of the water, but in the end it didn't matter to Lisa. What mattered was that she had a wonderful time playing in the surf and then enjoying her picnic.

While her parents rested after lunch, she and Ben took a walk on the beach. He showed her different shells and told her the animals' names. For a few of them, he even included recipes! By the time they reached the rock outcrop that defined the end of the beach, Lisa's hands were filled with shells. So were Ben's. When they returned to the picnic site, they found Mr. and Mrs. Atwood packing up. The afternoon sun was beginning to dip toward the western horizon. It was time to go back to the hotel.

They were all quiet on the return trip. Lisa watched the banana groves, wondering once again at the fact that the bananas grew up instead of down, as she'd always assumed. She thought about all the marvelous things they had seen and done that day. She sifted through her newly acquired rocks and shells. She thought about all the things they had learned from Ben. She remembered all the beautiful sights they'd seen—so unlike anything at home, or even anything at their hotel.

Everything seemed to have taken on a sort of dreamy, unreal quality as they passed through the island's little villages, now almost familiar to Lisa. It was as different as anything she'd ever seen. It was far away from anything that had ever worried her. She'd had a wonderful day. Before she knew it, her eyelids drooped and shut and she fell asleep.

Lisa jerked awake as they hit the first speed bump entering their hotel's grounds. There were the tennis courts, the windsurfing beach, the practice putting green, the basketball court, the dining villa, and—Lisa gulped—some riders returning to the stable.

She'd forgotten all about the stable. She'd spent a

whole day not even thinking about Jill, Frederica, Velvet, and Jasper. She hadn't thought once about her bruises and her riding. She hadn't even thought about what she was going to do the next morning when she was scheduled to go on another trail ride, and she didn't want to think about those things now, either.

Lisa occupied herself with helping Ben unload the remains of their picnic, folding towels, and brushing sand off the beach ball and Frisbee. The Atwoods said their good-byes to Ben. Lisa gave him a little hug and thanked him for everything he'd done to make their tour of the island wonderful. He told her it had been his pleasure and she believed him.

Ben drove away then, so Lisa and her parents picked up all their things to take them to their rooms. While they waited for the elevator, Jill came by with another girl about her age. Lisa waved to her. "Hi, Jill," she said. Jill barely glanced at her. When she was a few steps away, Jill put her arm across her new friend's shoulders and began whispering in her ear. The other girl glanced at Lisa, then turned back to Jill. The two of them started giggling. Lisa was sure she knew exactly what they were giggling about. She didn't like it at all. She could feel the wonderful relaxed feeling of the day drain from her as the two girls skipped in the opposite direction.

LISA MANAGED TO avoid Jill for the rest of the day and the evening, but she wasn't able to avoid the subject of horseback riding.

"What's that bruise?" her mother asked, looking at Lisa's shoulder as they sat at dinner that night.

Lisa had almost forgotten it because it was on the back of her shoulder and she hadn't been able to see it when she'd gotten dressed for dinner.

"What bruise?" she asked innocently, stalling for time. She had no idea what she wanted to tell her parents.

"The big purple patch on your shoulder, Lisa," her father said in a tone that indicated he didn't believe her innocent posture.

"Oh, that happened yesterday—" she began cautiously.

"You got hurt riding, didn't you?" Mrs. Atwood accused her. "I knew it would happen. We have to find out when the doctor is in."

"Oh, Mother," Lisa said, exasperated. "It's just a bruise. It's nothing."

Her parents regarded her suspiciously for a few minutes while they all ate in silence.

"It's not nothing," her father said after a while. "Why don't you tell us about it?"

Lisa knew then that she'd have to tell everything. When her mother blustered, Lisa could ignore it, but when her father asked her a straight question like that, she had to answer it.

She began at the beginning, explaining what had happened both days on the trail, how she'd fallen off twice and gotten the bruise the second time. Her parents waited patiently through the whole story, not interrupting once. But as soon as she was finished, her mother had a lot to say.

"I knew it—I just knew it. Horseback riding just isn't a safe thing for you to do. I'm sorry I ever encouraged you to do it in the first place. I had no idea it could be so dangerous. You're only bruised now, but soon you'll be coming home with broken bones and then heaven knows what."

"Mother," Lisa said, trying to sound patient, "I never had one teeny bit of trouble with getting hurt or being thrown at Pine Hollow. They know I'm a good rider and they trust me and I seem to ride better there."

Mrs. Atwood nodded. "Well, of course, any place that Mrs. diAngelo lets her daughter ride is going to be the very best. I'm sure they have nothing but well-behaved horses and everything is done for your safety. We just can't trust the horses and instruction at a stable we don't know. That's it. There will be no more riding for you while we're here, and when we get home, we'll think about whether you can ride at Pine Hollow."

A week earlier, those words would have made Lisa very angry and hurt and she would have argued strongly with her mother. But now she didn't say anything. After all, she was a good rider, so the fact that she'd fallen twice on San Marco had to be somebody else's fault. Maybe it was Velvet's jerkiness; maybe it was Jasper's lumbering gait. *Or maybe,* she thought dispiritedly, *I'm really just not as good as I thought. Maybe Mom's right. Maybe I shouldn't ride anymore at San Marco and then when I get home, well, I'll think about that then.*

"Don't you think so, Richard?" Mrs. Atwood asked.

Lisa's father was contemplating the seafood special in front of him. "I don't know, Eleanor. I don't think forbidding Lisa to ride is a good idea. Lisa, I don't want you to get hurt, but aren't you supposed to climb back on a horse when you fall off?"

"I did, Daddy. I finished the ride. But maybe"—Lisa hesitated—"maybe Mom's right."

"Maybe," he said, and then ate a shrimp.

7

THE GLOOMY GRAY skies hung over the shopping mall, dimming the last vestige of winter sun. As far as Stevie was concerned, the weather almost perfectly matched her mood. This was the end of her second day of shopping at the mall, and it had been no better than the first. She was practically talking to herself as she stood by the bus stop, waiting for the bus that would take her to the shopping center in town, from which she could walk home. It felt as if it would take forever until she could be in her own room, away from rude salespeople and masses of shoppers rushing everywhere.

By her own count, she'd been into every store in the mall that sold clothes for females, including a shop for senior citizens and three jeans specialty shops. That just showed her level of desperation. She'd actually tried on a "golden-age special" at the senior citizens' shop, but even the saleswoman had to agree that it was "a little mature for you." The only thing the dress had going for it, in fact, was that it was blue.

The good news was that Stevie had found three dresses she could consider wearing to the New Year's Eve dance. That is, she could consider them, but she wasn't so sure that her mother would.

One dress was just beautiful. It was a glittery blue floor-length number. Its major drawback was the price. Stevie wasn't sure exactly how expensive it was. She'd noticed that the price tag had four digits to the left of the decimal, though, and she suspected her mother would think that was a bit too much to spend—for a car, to say nothing of a dress!

The next possibility was pretty, too. And the price was more reasonable, though still in the outrageous area. The problem was that once her mother saw it, she'd probably say just what the saleslady had said about the golden-age dress. It was a little mature for her, to put it mildly. This one was strapless, with a straight floor-length skirt slit halfway up her thigh. Of course, it was hard to get the full effect while she was wearing loafers and ankle socks, but she'd seen enough to know that her mother would let her wear a dress like that the day she turned, oh, say, twenty-five. If ever.

The final possibility was something Stevie could actually afford with a six-month advance on her allowance. It was a fancy dress and it was blue. The trouble was, it didn't fit properly and she wasn't sure she liked it. It had a babyish frilly neckline and puffed sleeves. It was made of layers of lacy fabric, all in different shades of blue and baby blue. The lace went around the puffed sleeves, too. Stevie was afraid it was all a bit too much, and she wasn't sure the style flattered her.

The bus pulled up to the stop and Stevie climbed on. Somehow, she wasn't surprised to find that she didn't have the right change and that nobody on the crowded bus could make change for her. She stepped back down again, knowing that she'd have to buy something to get the change, that she'd have to wait for the next bus, and that it would be even more crowded than this one. Stevie shook her head. It seemed like an appropriately rotten end to a rotten day.

"HOW'S IT GOING with Starlight?" Judy Barker asked Carole. The two of them were in Judy's truck, driving to a stable where, the owner had said, a horse was having a problem with his hoof. Judy was a veterinarian, and spending time with her meant learning that a lot of horses had hoof problems.

"It's okay," Carole said. "But it's such hard work. I mean, when it comes to learning something, Starlight is just like a little kid. It seems like we go over the same thing again and again and for a while, he'll get it, and then it's gone again."

"That's the way it is with horses, but it pays off in the long run. Once they've got something down, they've got it for good. Oh, occasionally they need reminders, but the earlier they learn, the better."

"And the younger I am, the better too. My legs are so

sore today from mounting and dismounting about five hundred times, I feel like I'm ninety years old."

"And that's a lot younger than you'd feel if he took off on his own while you were in the middle of mounting him sometime!" Judy joked.

Carole didn't laugh. She knew it was true. In the long run, all the work she was doing with Starlight was going to pay off. It was just that it was hard work and a little tedious, and at times seemed to be useless. What made it the hardest, though, was that it was lonely work. Lisa was off on her tropical island and Stevie was in her New Year's Eve dream world. It seemed that only Carole was left in the real world of horses, and she wasn't having much fun being there alone.

"Here we are." Judy swung her pickup into the driveway of the stable and was alighting from the cab before the engine had stopped turning. Carole tried hopping out the same way, but her thighs hurt too much. She muffled a groan and followed Judy into the stable.

The owner was nowhere in sight. Judy asked Carole to look for him. His name was Mulroney. Carole approached the house, on the other side of the stable's paddock, and found that Mr. Mulroney wasn't home. He'd left a note on his door for Judy, informing her that he'd had to go to town and would be back at four o'clock. If he missed her, she should check the right front hoof of the bay.

Armed with this information, Carole returned to the stable and told Judy. Judy put her hands on her hips and looked at the four horses in the stable. Three of the four were bays! Judy started laughing. Carole could only muster a wan smile. It seemed to her that what Mr. Mulroney was doing was selfish and thoughtless. She just couldn't bring herself to laugh about it.

"Okay, let's check them one by one," Judy said. "Try the stallion first. He's had hoof problems before and is probably the best candidate for trouble."

Carole approached the stall and knew right away that she didn't want to open the door. The stallion, whatever else might have been wrong with him, was in a foul mood. He was backed into the corner of his stall, his ears were flat on his head, and his eyes opened so wide, she could see white all around.

"Let's try the others first," Carole suggested.

Judy took one look and agreed.

The mare and the gelding were just fine, though, so they had to check out the stallion. Usually, Carole didn't mind whatever it was she had to do to take care of an animal. She was a horse lover and thought that meant she always had to be willing to do anything for the horse. It surprised her that she wasn't very willing in this instance. She was annoyed with her own discomfort from the tedious work with Starlight and she was annoyed with Mr. Mulroney, both for not being there and for not telling them which horse needed attention.

She was even more annoyed when, after a twenty-minute struggle to subdue the stallion, Judy discovered that his problem was a pebble in his shoe. She took the hoof-pick, pried gently until she found the culprit, scooped it out, and released the stallion's leg. He tested his weight on his foot carefully, and once he was assured that everything was back to normal, he began munching at his hay.

Judy filled out her paperwork and left a note for Mr. Mulroney.

"I bet he'll be embarrassed when he finds out what it was," Carole said.

"Not likely," Judy said. "It's happened before with this fellow. I think Mr. Mulroney is just willing to pay me to take out the stone because the stallion is so bad-tempered when he hurts."

"Some people are really weird!" Carole remarked. "Does someone who can't bring himself to remove a stone from his own horse's shoe actually deserve to own the horse?"

"Maybe not, but the horse is my patient," Judy reminded her. "I can't let my feelings about the owner interfere with my responsibility to my patient's health."

"No, of course not," Carole said. She understood; she just didn't like it. It surprised her to find that there were things about horse care and training that she didn't like. For a very long time, she'd always assumed that there wasn't anything to do with horses that wasn't wonderful. Now, she knew that wasn't exactly the case.

She was glad they only had three more stables to visit that day and they were all nearby. She was ready to go home, to soak in a hot bath and try to wash off all of her disappointment.

WHEN SHE FINALLY got home, Stevie took a can of soda from the refrigerator, piled seven Oreos onto a little plate, and made a beeline for her room. For once she didn't care that a snack like that could put all kinds of weight on her and make her too fat to fit into her lovely dream ball gown. As far as she was concerned, the ball gown in question wasn't a lovely dream anyway; it was a nightmare.

Stevie ate the Oreos in record time. The soda took a little longer, but not much. She brushed the crumbs off her lap and glared out the window. The whole thing didn't seem fair to her. She'd been looking forward to having a beautiful dress for the dance with Phil and she'd had nothing but misery from the moment she set foot in the mall—and that didn't even count the misery she was having trying to talk some sense into her mother! And, while she was doing that, what were her friends doing?

Her friend Lisa was on a beautiful tropical island, riding a strong, tall horse bareback through the surf of the turquoise Caribbean, probably being followed by a handsome young man, also an excellent rider. Maybe they were even riding at nighttime, with the moon and its shimmering reflection tracing their path along the beach, stretching across the waters to light their way to—Stevie didn't even want to consider where they were on their way to.

And then there was Carole. She had a beautiful new horse all her own. She was dividing her time between the wonderful world of animal medicine, where she was assisting Judy to save horses' lives, and training and riding her very own horse. Stevie could see Carole helping Judy as she tended to a gentle horse stricken by some terrible disease, the worried owner standing by. Carole would hand Judy the instruments and report on the horse's vital signs until the wonderful moment when the animal, now fully healed, could stand on its own and nuzzle Carole to thank her for saving its life. But that was just the half of it! Carole was also working with Starlight, perfecting his perfection. Stevie imagined the satisfaction Carole must be feeling as she taught him to respond to the slightest command—a weight shift, the minute movement of her heel, a twitch of her hands. She'd be garnering blue ribbons at every horse show in the county come spring.

Stevie reached for the plate. No more Oreos. She reached for the phone instead.

It only rang twice before Carole picked it up.

"You're home," Stevie said, surprised and pleased.

"Finally." Stevie thought she heard some relief in Carole's voice. That didn't make sense. She must have been mistaken. Before she could ask, Carole went on, "I've been thinking about you all day. Haven't you been at the mall?"

"Yeah," Stevie said.

"Did you find it—you know—The Dress?"

"Not yet," Stevie said.

"Oh, it must have been fun, trying on all those beautiful dresses!"

If only she knew, Stevie thought.

Carole continued, almost without pause, "I had this image of you finding exactly the right one, though, of course, in my image, I didn't figure out how you'd pay for it, but you'll find a way—you always find a way to solve problems like that—and I know whatever you pick, Phil is going to think it's just dreamy. You know what I saw on television last night? There was a girl going to a dance and she was wearing shoes that were just about invisible. I wonder if you could find any like that. Wouldn't it be something?"

"Sure would," Stevie said. "Especially if the price were invisible, too!"

Carole laughed. Stevie always had a way of finding something funny and wonderful, and no matter how tricky it could be to find exactly the right dress for the occasion, she knew Stevie would.

"I've been thinking about you, too," Stevie told her.

"You have?"

"Oh, sure, all the wonderful experiences you must be having with Judy, working with horses and their owners and, best of all, having the opportunity to work with Starlight as much as you want, teaching him good manners and tricks, and subtle signals and things like that. It makes such a difference if you know you'll be the only rider your horse ever has. You must be having a blast."

If only she knew, Carole thought.

"I wonder how Lisa's doing," Carole said, changing the subject.

"Fabulously, I'm sure," Stevie said. "I was just having this image of her—" She told Carole about her daydream.

"Sounds just like what would happen to Lisa," Carole said wistfully.

IF ONLY THEY *knew*, Lisa thought. She hadn't been able to get her mind off Stevie and Carole, knowing they were back home where things were right, and fun. Stevie was probably having a great time trying on every dress in the mall and would have no trouble finding the right one. And Carole was probably riding Starlight every day without worrying about who else would ride him and what might happen while somebody else was on him. He was hers, forever. How wonderful that was! And then Lisa thought about herself. Here she was, on this beautiful island having such an awful time, and wishing more than anything that she were home again or that her friends were with her. They'd make it fun for her. They always did.

Lisa lay in bed with her hands clasped behind her head, unable to sleep. The light of the full moon streaked into her room, but that wasn't what was keeping her awake. She was awake because she was confused. Then her mother's words began running through her head. *There will be no more riding for you while we're here.*

For a reason Lisa didn't understand, she found the words comforting. They solved the problem for her. She would stop riding for the rest of the vacation. With that thought, Lisa closed her eyes again, and slept.

THE PHONE BY Lisa's bed jangled loudly. She sat up with a start and stared at it, bleary-eyed, for a few seconds before answering it.

"Yes?" she said.

"Wake-up call," a voice said cheerfully. "It's eight-thirty." The cheerful voice hung up.

Lisa looked at her clock. The voice had been correct. It was eight-thirty. But why was it calling?

Then she remembered that she'd asked for the wake-up call during her whole stay so she could be up, dressed, and fed in time for the intermediate ride. But, of course, that didn't matter today because she wasn't going to go riding. She snuggled back down into her comfortable bed.

But she couldn't fall back asleep. Her mind filled with thoughts of horses.

She thought about Velvet and the mistake she'd made with the mare. It wasn't Velvet's fault, or anybody else's, that Lisa hadn't been looking where the trail went and had lost her balance. It was Lisa's fault. Failing to look ahead was a babyish kind of mistake, one that she shouldn't have made.

Then she asked herself what had gone wrong with Jasper. She thought about the incident and recalled how the change of speed had come as a surprise to her. It shouldn't have. She was looking ahead. She saw the water coming up. She knew the horse would have to slow down. How could she have missed that? It was as if she'd corrected the mechanics of the mistake she'd made on Velvet, without correcting the reason for the mistake. Basically, the same thing had happened to her twice, and until that minute, she hadn't learned a thing from it!

That was it. Her falls weren't her horses' fault; they weren't Frederica's fault, or Jill's, or anybody's but her own. She'd been so insulted by Frederica's doubt that she'd forgotten that horseback riding was work and required a rider's total attention—especially a rider who was as relatively new to the sport as Lisa was.

"I *am* a good rider," she said out loud. "But only when I do the things I've learned. When I forget all my lessons, I'm no better than the greenest beginner."

Lisa had a painful moment remembering Jill's snickering the evening before. No one had ever snickered about anything she'd done in her life. It had hurt. But the more she thought about it, the more she saw Jill's point of view. To Jill, Lisa must have looked like a conceited jerk. She'd talked about all her lessons, her Pony Club, the gymkhana, the rodeo, her friends, and made herself look impressive, and then she'd managed to look like somebody who didn't know which end of the horse ate hay!

Riders could be cruel to one another. Lisa had seen that from time to time. People who were good at riding didn't tend to be tolerant of those who weren't. Even The Saddle Club had indulged in occasional laughs at new riders' expense. How could Lisa have expected Jill to react any differently from the way she did? Lisa had been riding like a fool. No wonder Jill had treated her badly.

She sat up in bed and looked at her clock. It was nine o'clock. Her parents had said they'd be playing tennis this morning. They would never notice if she went to the stable. For a second, Lisa thought uneasily of her mother's reaction to her bruises. Then she remembered that her father had disagreed with her mother. She wasn't actually forbidden to ride after all. But it was getting late. She'd have to hurry to get to the stable on time!

"AH, LISA, IS it?" Frederica greeted her. "Do you want to ride with us again?"

Lisa had skipped breakfast and arrived at the stable a full half hour before the trail ride was set to begin. She was sure she'd need the extra time. She'd found Frederica in the stable, checking a gelding with a leg wrap. Lisa automatically reached up to hold the horse's halter while Frederica examined the leg.

Lisa took a deep breath. She had the feeling it wouldn't be easy to convince Frederica to let her come on the ride. After all, it hadn't been easy to convince her the first time and she hadn't done anything since then to make herself seem a better candidate for a successful trail ride.

"I need to do this, Frederica," she began. "See, I know I'm better than I've been showing you. I've spent a lot of time thinking about my mistakes and they were bad ones. At first, I thought it was the horses' fault, but it wasn't. Then, I tried to convince myself it was something you were doing, or Jill, or almost anybody else. The fact is, I've gotten awfully used to riding on one kind of terrain and I forgot to adjust to another."

She paused, expecting Frederica to argue with her, but Frederica was looking carefully at the leg for signs of reduced swelling.

"This leg is definitely getting better," Frederica said at last.

Lisa had seen swollen legs like that many times in the past. "Are you using DMSO?" she asked. That was a drug she'd seen Judy and Max use many times on sore and swollen legs.

Frederica looked at her sharply. "You do know about horses, don't you?"

"Not as much as I thought I knew the first day I arrived," Lisa admitted.

Frederica nodded. "Yes, you could be right about that. Well, help me put the bandage back on and let's talk about what we should do."

While Frederica painted the affected leg with DMSO, Lisa rerolled the leg wrap so Frederica would be able to replace it.

"What's been going wrong?" Frederica asked.

"I just haven't been paying attention," Lisa said. "Both times I fell, I wasn't prepared for changes—once in direction, the second time in speed."

"Did you get hurt? I mean *really*. And tell me the truth. I can't let you ride if you're not sound, any more than I could permit an unsound horse to go on the trail."

Lisa understood that. It would be totally irresponsible to let somebody who wasn't up to it physically go out on a trail.

"I've got a bruise on my hip that's all kinds of reds and blues. My knee took a kick and my shoulder is sore. But nothing's so sore I can't ride."

Frederica made Lisa show her the shoulder and knee bruises and agreed that they were certainly uncomfortable, but not disabling.

When Frederica was finished with the horse's leg, she and Lisa went to the office to see who else was going to be on the ride and to see how they could make the experience safer for Lisa.

"Jill's coming back, of course," Frederica said, glancing at the list. "She rode yesterday, as well, and made some unkind remarks about you."

"I deserved them," Lisa said matter-of-factly. Frederica didn't comment further.

"Okay, then, here's what we'll do," she decided. "I'm going to put you on Jasper again. He can be slow, but he's responsive."

"I know," Lisa said. "He's gentle and doesn't have much of a mind of his own."

76

"Just so," Frederica agreed. "I'm also going to put you in a Western saddle. Have you ridden Western?"

"Yes, I have," Lisa said. "And that's fine with me. This is sort of a comeback ride for me. I ride English most of the time, but a Western saddle will give me more support."

"And something to hang on to if you need it," Frederica added, referring to the Western saddle's pommel, originally intended to hold a cowboy's lariat. Greenhorns used it as a handle.

"I won't need it," Lisa said.

"I hope not," Frederica told her. "But it's there if you do."

"Okay," Lisa said.

She'd done it. She had convinced Frederica to let her ride again. At first, that had seemed like the only obstacle she'd have to overcome, but as she emerged from Frederica's office, Lisa realized that it was the least of the problems she had to deal with.

There, standing patiently in the shade of a palm tree outside Frederica's office, was Jasper, a Western saddle being placed on his back. He seemed as calm as he had been on the first day she'd seen him, munching on strands of grass, awaiting the inevitable daily trail rides he'd come to expect, and endure. That seemed to be the way Jasper felt, but it wasn't the way Lisa felt. Suddenly, in a way she had never known before, she was terrified. Jasper was big, very big. He seemed like the biggest horse she'd ever seen. If she fell from him . . .

Jill's voice interrupted her thoughts. "Why, Lisa,

you're back?" she said. "Are you going to sign up for the beginners' ride?"

"No," Lisa said calmly, "I'm going out on the intermediate ride again. That's what I am—an intermediate rider."

"Oh. I thought you were an *expert,* you know, the way you talked about your lessons and your club and everything."

The scorn in Jill's voice was unmistakable. Lisa had no choice but to confront it directly. "I guess that's because I made it sound that way," she admitted. "I'm not an expert. But I *am* an intermediate."

"I guess we'll see, won't we?" Jill asked.

"I guess so," Lisa said.

Jill turned her back on Lisa and prepared to mount her horse. Lisa turned back to Jasper.

"Here, I'll help you mount," said Alain, the stableboy. Lisa knew he'd been sent over by Frederica and decided that she could probably use the help. The fact was, she was shaking so much she wasn't sure she could get into the saddle without help.

9

FREDERICA GAVE THE signal and the horses began to move. Once again, Lisa was the second-to-last person in the ride. She was glad for that, because it meant only one person could see how badly she was shaking, and if she fell off, only one person would watch her do it.

She gripped the big saddle with her legs as tightly as she could. She held the reins with both hands, clutching the pommel of the saddle at the same time. The reins were quite loose, and she permitted Jasper to do pretty much what he wanted, following the horse in front of him. For now, that was okay with Lisa. If she didn't have to tell him what to do, he couldn't disagree with her.

She knew, beyond any doubt, that this was a bad way to ride. Carole and Stevie would be the first ones to tell her so, and Max would be yelling instructions at her so fast, it would be everything she could do to hear them, much less follow them. Still, at that moment, she was doing the best she could, and that was enough.

"Prepare to trot!" Frederica called out. Lisa gulped. Trotting meant taking control of her horse. She couldn't have Jasper going at a trot without having the reins work for her. Carefully, she tightened up on the reins, barely releasing her grip on the pommel. By the time Jasper began his lumbering trot, Lisa was holding the reins properly. She rose slightly in the saddle to post. Usually, she knew, riders didn't post in a Western saddle, but Lisa felt more comfortable doing it, so she posted.

Posting, she found, was a good thing to do. Since it involved shifting her weight to match the rhythm of the horse's trot, it helped to remind her about balance. She'd been so upset over her riding experiences the last few days, she'd forgotten how important balance could be. A balanced rider could do anything. An unbalanced rider was hopeless. Posting helped Lisa to find her own balance.

As they approached the beach, the horses slowed to a walk. Lisa found herself more relieved than she thought she had the right to be. Was she relieved that she'd actually made it through a trot? Not really, she decided. She was more relieved that she was finding she was enjoying the ride.

"Good work," a man's voice came from behind her. "You're really a good rider, aren't you?"

"Not really," she said over her shoulder, wondering what Frederica had said to the poor man by way of preparation.

Frederica raised her hand. "Prepare to canter!" she called out.

In spite of her earlier promises not to touch it, Lisa gripped the pommel so tightly that her knuckles turned white.

The horse in front of her picked up his pace to a trot and then to a canter. Jasper, trotting willingly, strained at his bit. He was ready to go. Lisa continued to hold the reins taut. Her horse might be ready, but she wasn't sure she was.

She heard the rider behind her cluck to his horse, urging him to a canter. She couldn't keep him back. She had to get going. Jasper trotted faster. His smooth trot was a very nice gait. She could even sit it, but for how long? She couldn't really go on for the rest of her life pretending she was cantering when she was actually trotting.

Her foot slid back on Jasper's belly, touching him behind the girth. At the same time her hands gripped the pommel more tightly, if that was possible.

Jasper responded immediately to her signal, rocking his head and changing his gait to a canter. Lisa gripped the horse firmly with her legs, but didn't hold him in the viselike grip she'd used on her last ride. She had to hold her legs steady, and the best way to do that was to hold her horse firmly. She loosened the reins, letting Jasper know that what he was doing was right.

Lisa looked forward. The trail followed the curve of the beach, and the horses splashed in the shallow tongues of surf. It was much easier for horses to canter on the wet section of the beach than on the dry sand, where their hooves sank into the softer footing. Jasper seemed to appreciate it. In fact, Jasper seemed to love it, almost coming to life on the beach. Lisa could feel his speed under her, but, thankfully, she didn't feel out of control. She moved one of her fingers on the right rein ever so slightly and Jasper immediately flicked his right ear to her. It was a sure sign that he was paying attention to her. At the same time, he clearly loved his canter by the sea. She smiled to herself. Jasper was a real sea horse. Now, she realized, since he was letting her take charge, she had to be worthy of his trust.

She sat deeply in the saddle, sliding forward and back easily with the one-two-three beat of Jasper's canter. Like most horses' canters, it had the feel of a rocking chair— moving fast, of course. Lisa looked up ahead and watched where Frederica swung her horse to the left to the part of the trail that led into the wooded area. It was the scene of Lisa's first tumble. The other horses on the trail ride followed. So did Jasper, when Lisa signaled him.

The horses slowed to a walk. Lisa felt relief, but there was more than that. She also felt comfortable. She was in the saddle of a gentle, responsive horse, riding through what surely had to be one of the prettiest trails in the world. She began to relax and enjoy herself.

Frederica led the riders up the curvy trail that snaked up to the hilltop. On the straightaway they cantered again, this time through the open field up toward the promontory. Now that Lisa knew something about the formation of the island, she had a better understanding of what the promontory was. It was a piece of land built up from the center of the island by a volcano, and cut back at the island's edge by the sea. She and her parents had seen several more of them on their trip with Ben. There was something about being on horseback, between the work of a volcano and the work of the ocean, that made Lisa feel very close to the heart of San Marco. She liked the feeling. Once again, she noticed Jill shy away from the promontory. Jill definitely didn't like heights.

The horses then descended down into the palm grove, once again passing the shabby little farm. The boy Lisa had seen before was by the side of his house, scattering grain for the chickens. Lisa waved to him. He waved back.

"Prepare to canter!" Frederica called.

Lisa was prepared. This time, she signaled Jasper to canter the instant the horse in front of her began to move faster. He changed gaits easily. She changed her seat and her hold on the reins, and he responded. She rocked with his motion. Riding was as easy as it had always been.

It had rained hard the night before and the small marsh that had caused Lisa such trouble two days ago was now much more perilous. The water was six inches deeper than it had been. Jasper slowed noticeably as he slogged through the water, but Lisa was prepared. She slowed, too. And she stayed on.

"Nice work," the rider behind her said. Lisa just nodded at the compliment.

Frederica led the riders through another palm grove,

around a grassy hillock, and back to the beach. Lisa could hardly wait for what she knew would be the final canter of the ride. Jasper seemed to sense her excitement. She certainly sensed his. As soon as they reached the beach, Frederica started the canter. Lisa was completely at ease, completely comfortable, and completely confident. Jasper was completely wonderful. The wind off the sea picked up his mane so that it blew back, accentuating his speed. The same wind brushed Lisa's hair, even under her helmet, and Lisa felt as if she were flying. She no longer felt any fear or apprehension. She only felt joy.

"Good work!" the rider behind her said. "I don't know what Jill was so worried about. You're just fine."

"I guess I am, now," Lisa said, smiling to herself at his words. It hadn't been Frederica who had warned the man behind her; it had been Jill. Frederica really *did* have faith in her.

That thought was confirmed a few minutes later when Frederica rode back along the line, pausing by Lisa.

"I knew you could do it, Lisa. Nice work."

"Thanks," Lisa said. "For your confidence in me, I mean."

"You're welcome," Frederica said. "But I'm not sure I ever really doubted you were an intermediate rider. Oh, I might have in the very beginning, when you told me you'd only ridden for six months. But you seemed to doubt yourself more than I did, and that was much more worrisome than if I'd doubted you."

Lisa knew that was true and she thought about what

she might have missed if she'd kept on doubting herself. It made her lean forward and pat Jasper affectionately on the neck. After all, he deserved thanks, too.

"Jasper helped, you know," Lisa said.

Frederica nodded. "He loves the ride, especially the beach. Did you notice?"

"I did," Lisa said. "He's a real sea horse." Frederica laughed, patting Jasper herself.

The riders all walked their horses the last quarter mile to the stable. Lisa would have liked to canter again, now that she knew she could really do it, but she also knew that horses had to walk to cool down. As they approached the stable, Jill drew her horse up, and waited for Lisa to catch up. "Stayed on this time, huh?" Jill asked rather snidely.

Lisa thought she was being unnecessarily nasty, but she wanted to give Jill the benefit of the doubt. "I'd just forgotten some of my basics," she said.

"Right, like staying on," Jill snickered.

"Yes, like staying on," Lisa agreed, trying to make fun of her own shortcoming. Then she realized it wasn't worth the effort. Jill was enjoying putting her down. That, Lisa decided, was Jill's problem, not hers.

Jill kicked her horse, urging him forward. He picked up a trot and was soon back at his own place in the line of riders. Lisa wasn't sorry to see Jill gone.

Although they had walked the horses a full quarter mile, Jasper was still lathered and breathing hard by the time they got into the mounting and dismounting area. He wasn't ready to stop walking until he was fully cooled down. His condition concerned Lisa enough that when Frederica came to help her dismount, Lisa pointed it out to her.

"I think I should walk him some more, don't you?" she asked.

Frederica regarded him carefully. She nodded. "I agree. Why don't you take him into the ring and circle it for another ten minutes or so."

Lisa rode Jasper over to the schooling ring, where he could cool down at his own pace. She reached over and unlatched the gate and then latched it behind her. Relatching it was habit more than anything else. Max had drilled the idea into his riders' heads that any gate that had to be opened also had to be closed.

Jasper was comfortable circling the ring and Lisa was comfortable remaining in the saddle. She decided to ride him at a walk for five minutes and then lead him for the next five. Besides, that method would give her five more minutes of riding time.

She kept Jasper on a loose rein and let her mind wander as they walked gently in large lazy circles.

She was riding again. That was the most important thing. She was good and she felt good. The only thing missing was that her friends weren't there to enjoy the victory with her. Stevie and Carole would have understood everything. In fact, she was sure that if Stevie and Carole had been there, the whole mess wouldn't have happened in the first place. They would have known what was wrong before Lisa did and they would have gotten Lisa to correct it before it had gotten her in so much trouble. One of the nicest things about Stevie and Carole was that they were friends no matter what. It was too bad she couldn't say the same for Jill.

10

LISA HAD ONLY gone halfway around the ring before trouble started. This time, it wasn't trouble for her. It was trouble for Jill.

Lisa heard one rider scream while the man who had been behind her on the trail yelled, "Look out!"

She turned and instantly saw the danger. Jill had been in the process of dismounting from her horse when a breeze had shaken a coconut loose from the palm tree overhead. The large green fruit tumbled down, heading right for Jill's horse, Tiger!

Jill's right foot was out of the stirrup and her leg was halfway over to the horse's left side when the coconut struck Tiger on his rear. He jumped back first, then reared, nearly tossing Jill into the muddy dismounting area. That would have been all right. But, because Jill was a good rider, she somehow managed to get her right leg back over the horse and then she leaned forward, grasping for the horse's mane while he reared.

Lisa could see Jill clutching at Tiger's mane and realized that she'd lost control of the reins. They had slipped over her horse's head and there was no way Jill could reach them. Without the reins to check him, the terrified horse would run wild!

He took off like a flash, speeding past the schooling ring where Lisa was riding. A horse as scared as that could run for a long time, and on an island formed from volcanoes, there were a lot of places he could get into trouble. Lisa was barely aware of Frederica's dash for her own horse. The only thing she really knew was that she was the closest person to Jill and she might be the only one who could save her from a real disaster.

Her eyes flashed to the schooling ring gate, now so carefully latched. There was no time for niceties. There was no time for gates.

As quickly as she knew how, Lisa turned Jasper around and aimed him for the fence.

"Hyaa!" she said, slapping him with the end of her reins, since she wasn't carrying a crop.

Good old Jasper responded instantly. He broke into a spirited canter, dashing toward the fence and then, at just the right moment, Lisa leaned forward, rose in the saddle, gave him rein and let him fly over it! Behind her, she could hear some of her fellow trail riders applauding. It wouldn't mean anything, though, if something happened to Jill. She pressed on.

Jill and Tiger were about twenty yards ahead of Jasper.

That was a lot of ground for a tired horse to make up, but Jasper didn't seem tired or winded anymore. Instead, he seemed to understand the stakes and relished the chance to catch up with Tiger.

Lisa had become familiar with most of the riding area around the hotel, but that wasn't where Tiger wanted to go. He headed almost parallel to the beach, toward the small hilly peninsula that marked the far border of the hotel property. Jasper and Lisa followed. Lisa could see that Jill wasn't about to fall off. She was gripping tightly with her legs and had even gotten her right foot back into the stirrup. She clutched the horse's mane with her fingers. She was a good rider and would stay put.

"I'm coming," Lisa called out to reassure Jill, but Jill just screamed in response. Lisa decided to concentrate on the job in front of her, and reassuring herself instead of Jill.

She had one thing going for her in the rescue effort. Tiger zigged and zagged. It made it harder for Jill to stay on him, but it helped Lisa and Jasper. Every time he double-switched, they could gain a little on him. The problem was that the terrain was rough and rocky. At one point, Jasper stumbled. Lisa held on tight. Jasper righted himself and kept on going.

"Good boy," Lisa said.

Then, as suddenly as he had bolted, Tiger disappeared from view. At first, Lisa thought he'd just gone around a bend and she'd see him as soon as she turned the corner, too, but when she got there, there was no sign of Tiger or Jill. She pulled Jasper to a halt and stopped to consider and listen. As she did so, she could see Frederica coming up the hill behind her—on foot! She was leading her horse, who was limping noticeably. Lisa realized that he must have wrenched an ankle galloping over the rough terrain. There was no time to wait for Frederica to catch up. Lisa held her hand up to signal Frederica the direction she was taking so Frederica could follow.

The trouble was, Lisa didn't really know where to go herself. Jill and Tiger seemed to have disappeared altogether. Lisa hated to think what that might mean, and her worst fears were realized in the next instant when she heard Jill scream, "Help!"

Lisa kicked Jasper and diverted him toward the scream. The first thing she saw was Tiger, but Jill was no longer in the saddle. The horse was munching contentedly at some forest ground cover, apparently unaware of the trouble he'd caused. Lisa leaned over, picked up his reins, and twisted them around a nearby branch to keep him still until they found his rider.

"Jill? Where are you?" Lisa called out.

"Help!" she replied. "I'm here by the cliff, and I'm afraid I'm going over!"

Then Lisa spotted her and she didn't like what she saw. Lisa had thought they were on a hill on the peninsula, but when she looked more closely, she realized that it really wasn't a hill, it was a promontory just like the one on the trail. Jill was standing right on the edge, facing away from Lisa and frozen with terror as she stared down, mesmerized by the rocky ocean shore a hundred feet below her. She had obviously been thrown by Tiger and had ended up at the worst possible place for someone who was afraid of heights—the edge of the cliff. The wind buffeted the frightened girl, brushing her hair straight back, and whipping at her cotton blouse.

"I'm here," Lisa said. "Stay calm." She had to speak loudly to make her voice carry in the wind, but it didn't make much difference whether Jill heard her or not. Staying calm wasn't something Jill could do right then and Lisa knew it. The girl's fear of heights was now dangerous! Jill was simply paralyzed. She didn't appear to be in any immediate peril as long as she didn't step forward, but she didn't look capable of stepping backward.

"Can you sit down?" Lisa suggested, hoping that if Jill could at least lower her center of gravity, she'd be less likely to lose her balance.

"I can't move," Jill said. "I'll fall if I move. I know I will."

"Then stand still," Lisa advised, knowing it was the only advice Jill could take right then. It didn't do much to improve the situation, but Lisa hoped it might buy her some time.

What she needed was rope, but there wasn't any. She glanced wistfully at the pommel on Jasper's saddle, wishing a lariat would magically appear. As she thought about it, though, she realized she didn't really need rope. What she needed was something Jill could hold on to that would give her confidene. In reality, there wasn't a reason in the world that Jill couldn't step away from the edge of the cliff. In Jill's mind, there were a hundred reasons why she couldn't do it, and all of them were fears leading straight down to the ocean below.

Lisa's mind raced. She wanted something long and strong. Something familiar and comforting to Jill. Then she got it.

"I'll be back with help," she told Jill. "Stay there, okay?"

Jill didn't even answer. Lisa rode back the few yards to where she'd secured Tiger and, as quickly as she ever had, she removed the horse's bridle. Tiger, tired out from his uphill gallop, didn't seem to be inclined to run.

When Lisa and Jasper returned to the crest of the promontory, Jill hadn't budged. Lisa approached her carefully.

"I'm going to give you something to hold on to," Lisa called to Jill. "One end is in your hand, the other is on the pommel of Jasper's saddle. It is strong and absolutely secure. Nothing can go wrong. Do you understand?"

"I'll lose my balance if I move my hand to take it," Jill said.

"You won't," Lisa promised her, hoping she was right.

She dismounted and hooked the bit end of the bridle onto Jasper's pommel. He stood absolutely still. Very carefully and very slowly, Lisa approached Jill, afraid that if she startled her, Jill would lose her balance. Lisa talked quietly and reassuringly all the way. She felt as if she were talking to a frightened horse who just needed to hear a calm voice, and then she realized she wasn't far wrong. Jill didn't respond to any of the words she said—not that

Lisa even knew what she was saying—but she did respond to the confident tone of her voice.

"Now, in just a few seconds, I'm going to reach out and place this in your right hand," Lisa said. "You won't even have to look. You'll be able to feel it. Then I want you to grip it as tightly as you can. After that, you'll feel it pulling you away from the edge, away from the danger, away from the ocean. Go with the pull, go away from the edge to safety. Do you understand?"

"Don't touch me. I'll fall," was all Jill said.

"I won't," Lisa promised.

When Lisa was as close as she could get to Jill without endangering herself on the edge, she reached for Jill's hand, stretching every muscle of her body and arm. At first, she didn't think she could do it. Then, with a final effort, she slid the leather into Jill's open hand. Jill's fingers grasped the leather and Lisa knew everything was going to be all right.

Lisa returned to Jasper. "Come on, fellow, your turn now," she said. She took his reins and tugged gently. He began moving very slowly, taking up the slack in the bridle that led from his pommel to Jill's hand. Lisa watched as Jill gripped the rein even tighter, her knuckles turning as white as Lisa's had at the beginning of the trail ride. It was a grip of fear.

Jasper moved back from the cliff, and when the rein became taut, just like magic, Jill stepped back away from the edge as well. All it took was three steps and Jill was on her own. Still clutching the rein, she spun around and ran away from the edge, straight toward Jasper, and straight toward Lisa.

Lisa grabbed her and hugged her. Jill was still shaking with fear.

"You're okay now," Lisa soothed her. "Everything is all right. You're going to be fine. Nothing bad is going to happen to you. You're safe. You're really safe."

Jill glanced back at the cliff only once and then she began crying. Lisa sat down on the grass. Jill joined her, sighing and crying with relief.

"Thank you," Jill managed to say between sobs. "I was so scared I couldn't move."

"I saw that," Lisa told her. "And I know how it feels. There's something that's really easy to do, but you're so scared you don't think you'll ever be able to do it. I knew that all you needed was a little confidence."

"That thick rope gave me all the confidence I needed," Jill said.

"That thick rope was just a thin piece of leather," Lisa said. "All the confidence you needed was already inside you. You just lost track of it for a few minutes." She waited for Jill to stop crying.

At last, Jill looked up at her. "I'm so ashamed," she said. "I owe you about a million apologies, as well as thanks—"

Lisa patted Jill on the shoulder. "If you really want to thank me, you can ride with me tomorrow."

"Would you want to ride with me now?" Jill asked.

"Of course," Lisa said.

They were interrupted by Frederica's arrival.

"What's going on here? Are you both okay?" Frederica asked, bringing her horse to a stop. She gazed curiously at the two girls sitting in the grass fifteen feet from the edge of the promontory.

"Oh, we were just admiring the view," Lisa said easily.

For a second, she thought Jill was going to start crying again, but Jill swallowed hard and managed a weak smile. "It's a once-in-a-lifetime experience," she told Frederica.

Lisa began giggling then, and Jill joined her.

Frederica shook her head in disbelief, but Lisa was sure she was smiling at the same time.

11

"CAN YOU BELIEVE it's only two more days to the dance?" Phil asked Stevie on the phone. "I tried to call you yesterday and the day before, but no one answered. Where were you?"

"I've been at the mall," Stevie said. "The fact is, I've been looking for the right thing to wear on New Year's Eve and I haven't found it yet. I'm looking for something blue, you know." She was sitting on her bed as she spoke, the phone held up with her shoulder, and applying clear polish to her nails. Her dress would probably be a disaster. The least she could do was make her nails pretty.

"I guess I'm lucky," Phil said. "I got my outfit for Christmas."

"You did?" Stevie asked, very surprised. She didn't remember him mentioning anything about a suit or tuxedo under the tree.

"Sure, remember? I told you—"

She didn't remember anything of the sort.

"—the sweater my mother knit for me. It's blue, so it should go nicely with whatever you get. I'll wear that, and a white button-down shirt and some khaki pants and loafers, and that should do it."

Stevie gulped. She was beginning to get the impression that somebody had made a big mistake about the dance and that somebody was her. "For the dance on New Year's Eve that I'm going to with you?" she asked, just to be sure.

"Well, for supper first at my house, too. You can come early for that, can't you?"

Stevie could barely squeeze the words out. "I'll ask my parents what time they can bring me," she said. "I'll call you tomorrow, okay?"

"Okay, but what's the rush?"

The rush was that Stevie couldn't believe what a colossal, awful, terrible, miserable, embarrassing mistake she had been making and she just couldn't say any more.

"Talk to you then," she said hurriedly, and then hung up the phone just in time before she gasped.

Sweater, khakis, and loafers? She had to call Carole right away!

Carole wasn't home. "She's over at the stable, working with Starlight. I bet she'd love some company, though," Carole's father said. Then, because he and Stevie always enjoyed trading silly jokes, he gave her his latest one. "Did you hear about the Marine who saved his entire regiment?" he asked.

Stevie was beyond silly riddles at that point. She desperately needed to see her friend.

"No, tell me another time," she said, and then found herself hanging up on Colonel Hanson as quickly as she'd hung up on Phil. There was just one thing on Stevie's mind and that was talking to Carole. Carole was almost the only person in the world to whom she could confide the horrendous blunder she'd almost made.

Stevie hopped off her bed, slipped on her barn boots and her down jacket, and headed for Pine Hollow.

As Colonel Hanson had said, Carole was out in one of the paddocks talking sternly to Starlight.

"Whoa, there, Starlight. Stand still," she said. Then, when the horse was motionless, she mounted him and patted him. "Good boy," she said.

"Hey, you've gotten him to stop stepping forward when you mount him!" Stevie said with genuine admiration. "Nice trick!"

"But not an easy one," Carole told her. "And just because he behaved this time, it doesn't mean he won't misbehave the next time. Judy says that's the way it is with horses. You just have to keep working and working and telling and telling and then, eventually, they get it. Stepping forward when he was being mounted is a bad habit somebody let him develop. I have to break him of it. That is, if he doesn't break me first."

"Oh, you're doing wonderfully," Stevie said. "You always do wonderfully. You never make mistakes, especially when it comes to horses, and you've got all the patience in the world for them."

"That's what you think," Carole said. "I've been working so hard all week and it seems like I've barely accomplished anything! Well, I don't want to complain. You, on the other hand, have been trying on one fairy-godmother-type dress after another and having a blast at the mall."

"That's what you think," Stevie said.

"I thought you were having fun," Carole said, surprised at Stevie's tone of voice.

"And I thought *you* were having a blast," Stevie said. "Mostly, I've been wishing you and Lisa could help me and now . . . well, wait until I tell you what's happened."

"Before you do, why don't you go see if Max will let you take Topside out for a trail ride and we can talk while we ride. It sounds to me as if both of us need to take a break from what we've been doing and get down to what it is we like doing—namely, riding. I deserve it. Don't you?"

"You bet I do," Stevie agreed.

She found Max in his office, grumbling over some end-of-the-year paperwork. He told her she was welcome to ride Topside as long as she didn't work him faster than a walk on the frozen ground.

"No problem, Max," Stevie said. She was so exhausted from all her worrying that she didn't think she could go faster than a walk anyway.

It took only a few minutes before Topside was saddled and ready to go. She led him to the stable door, touched the stable's good-luck horseshoe, and joined Carole in the paddock. The two of them opened the gate, left the paddock, and closed it behind them.

"Let's go," Stevie said.

"Where to?" Carole asked.

"The woods," Stevie suggested. "I bet they're still covered with the snow that fell on Christmas Eve, and I bet they're beautiful."

"Deal," Carole said. "I'll lead the way. You talk."

Stevie fell in behind Carole and began telling her all about what had actually been going on at the mall, how the dresses were either ugly or expensive or, even worse, both.

"I didn't realize you were having such a tough time," Carole said sympathetically.

"Not that it mattered, though—"

"I know. Your mother wouldn't buy a dress for you anyway."

"Well, there's that, but that's not the worst of it." Stevie told Carole about her most recent conversation with Phil.

"Blue sweater, with a tux?" Carole asked, as confused as Stevie had been initially.

"Without a tux," Stevie corrected her. "With a white shirt, khakis, and loafers."

It finally sank in.

Carole's eyes widened. "You mean this isn't a formal dance? Is that what I'm hearing?"

"Roger, over, and out," Stevie said, imitating a radio operator.

At first, Stevie thought Carole was just speechless because she didn't say anything. Then, from her vantage point in the rear, Stevie became aware of the fact that Carole's shoulders were shaking in a very familiar manner. She was laughing!

"You're not laughing at me, are you?" Stevie asked, a little hurt.

"Of course I am!" Carole said between bursts of giggles. "And the reason I'm doing it is because the whole situation is ridiculous."

"It is?" Stevie said.

Carole couldn't answer her then; she was laughing too hard. Stevie began to think about it in a new light. At first, she had been angry that her daydream bubble of the blue chiffon dress and silver sandals had been burst by Phil's blue sweater, but as she thought about it, Carole was right. The situation *was* ridiculous.

Stevie laughed, too. "Can you see me in a blue chiffon dress that perfectly matches the sweater Phil's mother made? Maybe she makes sweaters for all these formal occasions. He'll get a black one for the senior prom, a white one for his wedding. And me? I'll just switch chiffon outfits!"

"Absolutely. You can get a chiffon riding outfit and a chiffon gym suit—oh, don't forget the chiffon bathing suit . . ." Carole gasped with laughter.

"I wonder what color sweater his mother will knit for that!"

Pretty soon, Stevie was giggling even harder than Carole. Their horses seemed a little confused by the hilarity.

Carole drew Starlight to a stop. Stevie pulled up next to her and they stayed there until they were in control of themselves.

"Oh, that felt good!" Stevie said, taking a deep breath of the cool December air. Along with the laughter, the air seemed to cleanse away all the misery and self-pity that had been building up in her for days.

"Phil must never know!" she said.

"Maybe on your fiftieth wedding anniversary," Carole suggested. "But before then, we have to decide what you're really going to wear."

Stevie scratched her head to help her think, forgetting that she was wearing a helmet. "I've got it," she declared. "If he's wearing blue, I should, too. I've got a blue-plaid skirt and a white sweater that goes with it. I can wear a turtleneck under that and I'm all set, don't you think?"

"Sounds good to me. Didn't you wear that when he came to your house on the Saturday after Thanksgiving, though?"

"I'll bet you anything he won't notice. There, that problem's been taken care of. Now, what's been bugging you?" Stevie asked.

"I think I've just discovered what hard work it is to train horses. And it seems to take forever until the work pays off. The thing I have to remember is that it *will* pay off, and in the end, it's worth it. But I've been so lonely."

"Me, too," Stevie said. "Malls are awful without friends."

"Stables aren't much better," Carole told her. She

started Starlight walking once again and the two friends rode on into the woods in contented silence for a while.

The woods were still filled with snow that made a squeaky sound as the horses trod through it.

"Look, the brook!" Carole said, pointing ahead.

There was the brook that they saw often in summer. There was a flat rock by its edge where they could sit and dangle their feet on hot, muggy days, cooling themselves from the bottom up.

"Let's stop for a minute," Stevie said. "I've got this sudden, incredible urge to make a snowball."

"Only you," Carole said, shaking her head in amazement, but she stopped and dismounted anyway. She noticed with more than a little satisfaction that Starlight stood absolutely still as she dismounted. She wrapped his reins around a thick bare branch and headed for the rock.

Stevie tied up Topside in a similar manner and followed Carole to the rock.

Stevie swept the snow off the flat rock onto her hand. She and Carole sat on the chilly rock while she formed the snow into a ball.

The creek in front of them was mostly covered with a thin crust of ice, though there were iceless patches and the girls could see the water rushing along underneath, as if it took no notice of the cold.

Stevie completed her snowball and tossed it back and forth from hand to hand.

"Is this a Saddle Club meeting?" she asked Carole.

"I guess any time we talk about horses and helping one another, it's a Saddle Club meeting, don't you think?"

"Maybe, but I miss Lisa."

"I do, too," Carole agreed. "But think how much fun she's having, doing nothing but lazing in the tropical sun and eating pineapples and coconuts."

"I bet she's bored," Stevie said.

"I bet she misses us," Carole said.

"Maybe as much as we miss her."

They sat quietly for a few minutes. Stevie was thinking about her friends and how much they meant to her. That reminded her of the abrupt farewell she'd delivered to Carole's father.

"Say, Carole, tell me about the Marine who saved his entire regiment. How did he do it?" she asked.

"You must have been talking to my father," Carole said. "Didn't he tell you the answer?"

"No, I hung up too fast. I just wanted to talk to you, then. So, how did he save the regiment?"

"He shot the cook."

"I can't *wait* until Lisa gets back," Stevie said.

"So she can tell us all about San Marco?"

Stevie grinned. "No, so I can tell her that awful joke!"

12

WHEN LISA WENT to her room to put on her dress for
dinner, she found a note slipped under her door. She
picked it up, put her towel on the cushion of the chair by
her mirror, and sat down to read. It was from Frederica.

"You are cordially invited to a private horseback-riding
picnic tomorrow. Come to the stable at eleven and wear a
bathing suit under your breeches."

That was all it said, and she couldn't wait to find out
what it all meant!

The next day, Lisa slept late, not getting up until almost nine o'clock. She met her parents down at the pool
and joined in on a game of water polo. At ten-fifteen,
she returned to her room, put on a dry suit, and put her
riding clothes over it.

Lisa met Jill on her way to the stable.

"Isn't this exciting?" Jill asked. "Just you and me and

Frederica. It's her day off from the stable, so she's taking us on a special picnic."

"We'll have a ball," Lisa said.

"Right, as long as we stay on the beach and don't go up on any of those cliffs." Jill couldn't help shivering.

"I'm pretty sure the reason we're wearing our suits is because we're going on the beach," Lisa said. Jill seemed relieved to hear the confirmation.

"Listen, I haven't thanked you enough or apologized for being such a jerk—" Jill began.

"Don't worry. I think I deserved it at least a little bit," Lisa said. "Besides, your being a jerk helped me get angry and that helped me figure out what was wrong. I should thank *you*."

Jill laughed. So did Lisa. It felt very good.

The last of the trail riders was leaving for the morning when Jill and Lisa arrived at the stable. Frederica greeted them both cheerfully.

"Are you ready for our party?" she asked.

"You bet!" Lisa said.

"Okay, then, Step One: your horses. Lisa, you pick first."

"Jasper, of course," Lisa said without hesitation. "He and I have been through a lot together."

"And *over* a lot together, as well," Frederica said. "If I recall, that included a four-foot fence."

"You *what?*" Jill asked, astounded.

"I had to get to you the fastest way," Lisa began.

"So she talked good old Jasper into going over that fence," Frederica said, pointing to the schooling ring.

Jill's jaw dropped. "I thought you were just beginning to jump," she said.

"I am," Lisa said. "And I guess I'm beginning to get the hang of it at the same time," she joked.

"Boy, I'm lucky you were there when Tiger took off."

"I think you were," Frederica agreed. "Lisa put on quite a riding display. But, now, speaking of riding, which horse do you choose, Jill?"

Jill thought for a moment. "Tiger, of course. We've been through a lot together as well. We had a great trail ride yesterday and, as long as we don't park him under any coconut palms, I'm sure he'll be fine."

"I thought so," Frederica said. She turned to the stable. "Alain, bring them out for the girls," she said. Alain emerged, leading Tiger and Jasper, all tacked up and ready to go. Frederica had known their answers before she'd asked them.

Lisa and Jill checked their tack and then mounted up.

"Let's go," Frederica said as soon as she was in the saddle of her own horse.

"Uh, excuse me," Lisa said, "but where's the picnic? Shouldn't we be carrying sandwiches or something?"

"Ah, no problem," Frederica said. "Alain is meeting us at the picnic place. It's his day off, too. He's driving the Jeep and he has to take the shortcut along the beach. Since we have the benefit of being on horseback, we get to mosey along the long way. Ready?"

They were.

Frederica led the girls and their horses on an unfamiliar trail. As with the trail they knew from the intermediate ride, it, too, changed terrain, from grassy field to palm grove to beach to brook to brush-covered hillside. And, it seemed to Lisa, every time they rounded a bend, they had another spectacular view of the stunning turquoise sea. Fortunately for Jill, none of those views involved being close to the edges of any cliffs.

"It's hard to believe I've only got two more days here," Lisa said wistfully. "I can't stand the idea of never seeing this again."

"It will be here when you come back," Frederica said. "And so will I." Lisa found that a very comforting thought.

The bridle path then led through the brush and down a hill toward the beach.

"We're picnicking at the far end of this beach. We can take a canter about halfway and then walk the final quarter mile. Ready?"

When they reached the hard-packed sand at the edge of the ocean, Frederica signaled for them to begin their canter. Lisa reached back with her heel and touched Jasper behind his girth on the left side. He responded instantly, as ready to go as she was. The ocean lay to her right, stretching endlessly toward the pale blue sky. To her left lay the whole island of San Marco, now almost familiar to Lisa. And ahead lay a long, lazy stretch of empty beach, white sand glistening in the bright sun. Its beauty nearly took Lisa's breath away.

Lisa barely thought about her riding. The setbacks of those first two days on the trail were behind her. Her body moved naturally with the gentle rocking of Jasper's

canter, and she adjusted her balance with the curve of
the beach and its slope to the water without thinking
about it. Jasper splashed almost playfully in the shallow
waves at the edge of the water. Lisa loved the sound. In
fact, she loved everything about this ride and so did Jasper, her very own sea horse.

From her very first lesson, Lisa had understood that
riding fast was not necessarily what riding was about.
Riding well was the most important thing. And riding
wasn't even necessarily the most important thing about
being with horses. Taking care of them properly meant
earning the right to ride. Still, there was a part of her
that loved a ride like this more than anything she'd ever
done with a horse. The breeze came in off the ocean
briskly. It brushed through Jasper's mane and her own
hair, sweeping it off her shoulders. For a moment, Lisa
imagined herself and Jasper as the sole inhabitants of San
Marco. They would live off the fruit trees and she would
ride every day. It would be wonderful.

At last the group rounded the point of the beach and
came upon another long crescent of sparkling white
sand. Lisa knew that this was the spot where they were
going to have their picnic. It had to be. Directly in front
of her were the strangest, most wonderful rock forma-
tions she had ever seen. The largest rock, which
stretched level from the side of the cliff to a distance well
out into the water, had a series of tall tunnels through it,
which gave it the appearance of having legs.

"We call this Aqueduct Rock," Frederica said, slowing
to a walk.

"I'm not surprised," Lisa said. Jill looked at her curiously. "It looks just like one," Lisa explained. "An aqueduct is an old-fashioned Roman water pipe, kind of like a bridge."

"There's a cave beyond it, too," Frederica informed them. "You can explore after we eat."

"Before we go swimming for the second time," Jill said.

"Third, maybe," Lisa suggested.

"Or fourth," Frederica added. "We're just here to have fun. Once the horses are taken care of, we can relax."

A few minutes later, they met up with Alain, who had parked the Jeep just off the beach on a dirt road. He had cool water and hay for the horses. Lisa helped him untack the animals and feed them while Frederica and Jill set up the picnic. Lisa was a little surprised by how much water Alain let the horses drink, but then she realized that she was in a tropical climate and the horses needed more water in hot weather like this than they did in the cooler weather at home.

"Race you to the rock out there," Jill said, challenging Lisa on her return to the beach.

"Hold up, there," Frederica said. "I have a few things to say first. Number one, sunscreen." She held out the bottle and saw to it that Lisa and Jill slathered on appropriate amounts. "Number two, although the water is calm here, these rocks can have some very sharp edges. Use your common sense and be careful. Number three, have fun."

With that, Frederica lowered herself onto her towel and began soaking in the warm sunshine.

Lisa and Jill ran to the water and splashed through the gentle surf until it was deep enough to swim. The rock outcrop they were racing to was about fifty yards away from the beach and almost seemed to grow out of the water. Lisa tried to imagine what kind of volcanic eruption would end up with that single rock fifty yards from the shore. By the time she'd arrived, she'd decided she couldn't know and it didn't matter; she was just glad it was there.

Jill was a good swimmer and beat Lisa to the rock. She found footing on the near side and climbed up carefully. Lisa followed close behind her.

The rock was mostly flat on top, though it was uneven enough to have indentations that formed little pools when the gentle waves occasionally splashed up on it.

"Look!" Jill cried out, gazing into one of the pools. Lisa joined her, crouching down on her haunches to look.

There, in about three inches of water, was what seemed to be a whole miniature world.

"There's an anemone!" Jill said.

"And look! A teeny crab!" Lisa said, pointing to a creature no bigger than her fingernail, scurrying through his small home.

Lisa shaded her eyes and searched through the little pool. She found some of the shells Ben had showed her. One, looking like a miniature turban with a pointed top, even had something living in it. "Some kind of snail, I think," Lisa said, observing the creature withdraw into its shell.

"And here are some mussels or something," Jill said, pointing to a section of the pool almost covered with tiny black half-open shells.

They spent another few minutes looking at the pool, and discovered that it had minnows living in it as well. Exploration of other tidal pools on the rock revealed more anemones, more crabs, some starfish, and even one brightly colored yellow fish, which seemed uncomfortable in the small amount of water. Very carefully, Lisa lifted it in her hand and tossed it back into the ocean. It was gone in an instant.

"I hope that was the right thing to do," she said.

"I know it was," Jill told her. "That fish was way too big for this little pool, and who knows when another wave would have come and given it a lift back to the ocean.

"Check this out," she added, pointing to a very odd creature crawling near another pool. It was a crab about the size of a quarter, and it had managed to cover itself with pieces of shell and rocks.

"My friend Ben told me about them," Lisa said. "They're called decorator crabs. Aren't they neat? And these animals over here are baby shrimp." She pointed to crescent-shaped creatures about half an inch long.

Jill giggled. "They look like barber poles. Look at the red-and-white stripes."

"I guess the red is supposed to camouflage them in cocktail sauce," Lisa joked.

When they finished exploring the tidal pools, it seemed like a good idea to go swimming again.

The girls examined the best way to get off the rock and then found something they thought many swimmers before them must have found as well. Halfway down to the water, on the side of the rock, there was a ledge that served as a perfect diving platform.

Lisa slipped into the water first to make sure it was deep and free of rocks. When she knew it was safe, she returned to the outcrop, climbed back up to the platform, and dived into the blue water. It felt wonderful.

Jill followed her in and the two of them raced back to the beach. This time, Lisa won. They toweled themselves dry and joined Frederica and Alain at the picnic site.

Both Jill and Lisa were famished. The picnic, prepared for them especially by the hotel kitchen, was wonderful. They ate it quickly, though, because there was still so much to do.

After lunch, Frederica and Alain showed them through the caves, which had been carved out of volcanic rock by eons of waves and tides. They weren't deep or scary caves, but they were lots of fun. Their floors were sandy while the walls and ceilings were craggy and rough. Lisa's mind slipped back to her daydream of living alone on the island with Jasper. She decided that if she did, she would definitely make a cave like this her home, unless—

"Does the tide still come in here?" she asked.

"Oh, yes," Frederica said. "In fact, this whole beach just about disappears at high tide, and that's at four o'clock today."

So much for her cozy home!

As they came out of the final cave, Lisa looked at the ocean and noticed the change. The rock she and Jill had swum to was now nearly submerged. The waves licked at the edge of the towel where they had sat for lunch. The beach was slowly being covered by water.

"How long have we got?" she asked.

Frederica consulted her watch. "We should leave in an hour," she said.

"Then we haven't got a second to spare," Lisa told Jill. "Let us know when a half hour is up and we'll help with the cleanup and tacking up, okay?"

"It's your celebration," Frederica said. "Spend the time as you wish. Alain and I can tend to the picnic leavings and the horses. I'll call you in an hour."

Lisa was glad they had a full hour, but it was clear that it wasn't nearly enough time to explore all the wonderful things there were to see on this beach. In the time left to them, they played hide-and-seek around the rock outcrops, including Aqueduct Rock; followed a land crab to his nest; watched the birds as they dove for lunch, emerging from the water proudly bearing fish in their breaks; and built a sand stable, complete with horses. Frederica's signal whistle came much too soon for Lisa. She was having a wonderful time with Jill, a time that could have been made better, she thought, only if Stevie and Carole had been there with her.

It had been a terrific day, and the ride back to the resort was almost as good as the ride to the beach. Lisa couldn't believe that because of some careless riding mistakes on her part, she had been willing to give it all up and never ride again. What a dreadful mistake that would have been!

STEVIE STOOD IN front of the full-length mirror in the bathroom admiring her reflection. It helped her ignore the fact that all three of her brothers were standing outside the bathroom door making kissing sounds.

The blue of her skirt went nicely with the dusty rose turtleneck and the white pullover. She sprayed on some sweet cologne and sniffed the air appreciatively. The final touch was the silver necklace Phil had given her for Hanukkah: a delicate horseshoe hanging on a herringbone chain. When she stepped back from the mirror, she could see the shoes her mother had bought her the day before. They were low-heeled navy blue pumps with silver buckles. She ran her comb through her hair a final time, blinked sweetly at her image in the mirror, and smiled. She liked what she saw. Full of confidence, she opened the bathroom door.

"Oh, Phil!" her older brother Chad teased, mimicking her. "You're *so* handsome!"

"Drop dead," Stevie suggested calmly, wafting past him and down the stairs to wait for Phil's arrival. "After all, who's going out on New Year's Eve? You or me?"

"THERE'S A BOGEY festival on tonight, Carole," Colonel Hanson said over dinner that night. "Want to watch some of it?"

Carole smiled to herself. She'd known for weeks about the marathon showing of Humphrey Bogart's movies. She'd also known that that would be how she and her dad would spend New Year's Eve. "Are you kidding?" she teased her father. "I already laid in a supply of microwave popcorn that will hold us through *Casablanca, Key Largo,* and *The African Queen.*"

"*The Maltese Falcon,* too?"

"Why not?" she answered.

As she and her father cleared the table, Carole thought about her friends. New Year's Eve was a special time and you should do special things on it. Stevie, for instance, was off to her dream dance with Phil. Lisa was doing whatever wonderful thing you did in the Caribbean on New Year's Eve. Carole thought that maybe she was luckiest of all. She loved to spend an evening just being with her father, even if it meant watching old movies with him, or maybe especially if it meant watching old movies with him.

"WE JUST HAVE fifteen minutes until the fireworks start," Jill said, looking at her waterproof watch.

"I still have to perfect my cannonball!" Lisa said, running down the diving board at the swimming pool. She paused at the end of it, jumped once to build up steam, and then a second time for effect. She bounded into the air, wrapped her arms around her legs, and made a loud splash as she landed. She rose to the top of the pool, looking up through the clear, fresh water with her goggles. It amazed her to realize she could actually see the stars from underwater. "Swimming at night is wonderful!" Lisa said.

"As long as there are some lights and it's a safe pool and there's a lifeguard," an adult voice said from above.

"Exactly," Lisa agreed. Then, as she swam toward the edge of the pool, she thought about other New Year's Eves she had spent. All of them, as long as she could remember, had taken place in Willow Creek and usually involved a small party her parents were giving. They had seemed exciting and grown-up to her when she was a little girl. Now that she was having a different kind of New Year's Eve, they seemed very boring.

"I think I want to do cannonballs and watch fireworks on San Marco for every New Year's Eve of my life," she said wistfully, pulling herself out of the pool.

"We could make a pact," Jill said. "I mean, as long as our parents will let us, we could always come back here for New Year's Eve . . ."

"Maybe," Lisa said, realizing that there was one thing missing—two really—Stevie and Carole.

*　　*　　*

"OH, DON'T YOU think he should have gotten on the plane, too?" Carole asked her father. She wiped a tear from her eye as she spoke. The end of *Casablanca* always made her cry.

"You're such a romantic!" Colonel Hanson said, teasing his daughter gently.

"Do you wish I weren't?" she asked.

"Nope. I think you're perfect the way you are. Besides, your mother always used to cry at the end of this movie, too. I think it must be something in the genes."

"And for that, it's your turn to make popcorn. I think you've got five minutes until the start of *The African Queen*."

Colonel Hanson took the empty bowl and soda cans to the kitchen. Carole thought she heard him humming "As Time Goes By" while the popcorn popped. It made her cry all over again. She loved it!

"DANCE?" PHIL ASKED, holding out his hand for Stevie to take.

"Of course," she said, accepting his invitation. "After all, if you were able to talk the committee into hiring a rock band, the least we can do is to dance to it."

The music started and they began dancing. Stevie liked dancing to rock music, but the trouble was, there was a lot of noise and she and Phil couldn't talk at all. She was pretty sure that eventually they'd play something soft and slow. Then, of course, she might not want to say anything! She smiled to herself.

"What's so funny?" Phil shouted, leaning toward her.

"Nothing in particular. I'm just having a good time," she yelled back.

"Me, too."

Then the music abruptly changed to a dreamy slow tune. Phil took Stevie's right hand in his left and pulled her toward him with his own right hand. She put her left hand on his shoulder, and they danced.

"I like rock, but this is nice, too," Stevie said.

"Hmmmm," Phil answered.

"How did you convince the committee to hire a rock band instead of the polka and square-dance groups they were considering?" Stevie wanted to know.

"It's a secret, see," Phil said. "We got this local rock band to offer their services for free. The parents' committee couldn't resist."

"The band is doing this for nothing?" Stevie asked.

"Oh, no, not at all," Phil said. "We passed a hat around to all the classes and paid the band ourselves. Our parents don't know it. They think they got a bargain. Considering the alternatives, we think we did, too."

"Very clever," Stevie said. "This sounds like A.J.'s work."

A.J. was Phil's best friend and he was almost as much of a schemer as Stevie was.

"It was his idea," Phil said. "And when he suggested it, I thought it sounded just like something you would have thought up."

Stevie laughed a little. Phil held her firmly, warmly. It was nice.

When the song was over, he suggested that they step

out in front of the gym where, though it would be cold, it would be quieter. Stevie agreed. He took her hand and led the way.

"You look wonderful tonight," he told her when they stood in the light by the door.

"Thanks," she said. "You're looking pretty terrific yourself."

"Your new outfit looks great. I know you spent so much time looking for it. I hope you had some fun doing it. I can tell you it was definitely worth it. The color is wonderful—and it goes so well—"

Stevie glanced down at her clothes to make sure they hadn't been transformed since the last time she'd stood in front of a mirror. Nope, there it was, the same old plaid skirt, dusty rose turtleneck, and white pullover. The light overhead was white. It hadn't even transformed the colors. She looked at Phil. He had an earnest and kind look on his face. He meant every word of what he'd said. Stevie did the only possible thing then. She said, "Thank you."

"Ooooh!"

"Aaaaaah!"

The fireworks burst into spectacular arcs of sparkling light and drifted down through the night sky. The crackling report of the rockets' gunpowder pierced the quiet tropical evening.

Lisa loved it. "Oh, look, red and blue and . . . gold! Can you believe the colors?"

Pfffstt. Another rocket left its launcher. This one

broke into long silver fingers that seemed to reach toward eternity and then began banging loudly like a string of firecrackers.

"Ohhhhhh!"

Lisa and Jill were stretched out on deck chairs by the poolside, a safe distance from where the fireworks were being shot off. They were wrapped warmly with towels over their bathing suits.

"This is the life," Lisa said, reaching for the tall glass of tropical fruit punch on the table beside her.

"I CAN NEVER decide which of these two characters I dislike more at the beginning or like better at the end," Carole remarked during a commercial break in *The African Queen.*

"Hmmm," her father said. "I never thought of it that way. I've just always liked to watch the transformation and the way they grow together. They're such an unlikely pair, aren't they?"

"Definitely an odd couple," Carole agreed. She stood up and stretched.

"You're not quitting, are you?" her father asked, a little concerned.

"No way," she said. "I'm here until Bogey's bitter end—or at least until midnight. I was just getting a little exercise."

"We can do aerobics between this and *The Maltese Falcon* if you'd like."

"No thank you, Colonel. This is a night off from things like that. Ready for another round of junk food?"

"Your turn," he said. Carole headed for the kitchen.

"WHAT TIME IS it?" Stevie asked, trying to look at Phil's watch.

He turned it around so she could see it. Eleven fifty-seven.

"It's almost midnight," he said, hugging her warmly.

"Yes, it is," she agreed, returning his hug.

They were back on the dance floor, pretending the band was playing slow music when it was actually playing rock music. Soon it wasn't playing anything at all.

The band leader turned to his microphone and announced that it was just two minutes to midnight—two minutes to a whole new year.

"I've kind of liked the last year," Stevie said. "There are parts of it that have been a lot of fun."

"Then I bet you'll like the new year even more," Phil said. She suspected he was right.

When there were only thirty seconds to go, the bandleader started counting backward. By the time he reached twenty, everybody had joined in. Stevie held Phil's hand and the two of them counted together.

"HAPPY NEW YEAR!" Lisa was with her parents when the social director of the resort informed them all of the passing of the old year and the arrival of the new. Both her mother and father gave her big hugs. She hugged them back. Jill came bounding over to them, squealing with excitement.

"Happy New Year!" she yelled. Lisa hugged her, too.

But what she was thinking about was Stevie and Carole.

HAPPY NEW YEAR

The words flashed across the bottom of the television screen, almost disappearing in the white water of the wild African river upon which Humphrey Bogart and Katharine Hepburn were being tossed.

"Happy New Year, Carole," Colonel Hanson said, standing up from his lounge chair to give Carole a New Year's hug and kiss.

"And to you, too, Daddy," she said, squeezing him hard. She loved her father and she couldn't think of anyplace in the world she'd rather be right then, but her mind was suddenly filled with two thoughts: Lisa and Stevie.

"SHOULD AULD ACQUAINTANCE be forgot
  And never brought to mind . . ."

Stevie was barely aware of the music and the singing around her. It was the first moment of the New Year and she was standing in the middle of the dance floor with Phil Marston, who had his arms around her and who was, at that moment, kissing her.

Her mind was too full of other thoughts to hear the song. All she could think of was Lisa and Carole.

14

"LIIIISSSAAAA!" STEVIE SHRIEKED as she dashed up the stairs at Lisa's house to her friend's room. "Was it fabulous?" She flung the door open. There, holding a pile of recently unpacked clothes, was a tan and happy Lisa.

"It was fabulous," Lisa informed her, dropping the clothes and hugging Stevie.

"I know it was. I got your postcard today!" Stevie produced it from her pocket. It seemed odd and distant to Lisa. It had been so long since she'd written that postcard. So much had happened.

"Hello? Hello?" Carole called from the Atwoods' front door and then followed Stevie's path upstairs, breathlessly calling out to Stevie and Lisa. "Don't tell anything until I get there!" She didn't want to miss a word.

Within a few minutes, Lisa's laundry was in the

hamper, her suitcase was put away, and the girls had a chance to talk—the first chance they had had in a week to have a Saddle Club meeting.

"You wouldn't believe this place, it's so gorgeous," Lisa began.

"The horses, were they okay?" Carole asked eagerly.

"One especially. His name was Jasper. At first, I thought he was sort of an old plug, you know, the reliable fleabag they put the beginners on, but then, when he had to get someplace fast—"

"What were you doing riding the horse they have to put the beginners on?" Carole wanted to know. It didn't surprise Lisa that Carole picked up on that.

"It's a long story," she began. And she told her friends everything that had happened. "In the end, it worked out all right, actually a lot better than all right because you wouldn't believe this place where we picnicked and what a wonderful feeling it is to canter along the seashore, but, oh, boy, I missed you guys! The whole thing would have been a lot easier if you'd been there to help me."

"I had exactly the same feeling," Carole said. "I was having a pretty hard time with Starlight. He's wonderful and all that, but the work was just better and more fun once Stevie had some time to help me."

Lisa looked at Stevie. "What were you so busy with that you—" Then she remembered. "Oh, your dress! What did you get? Tell me all about it! You must have had a blast at the mall."

"I'd almost forgotten," Stevie joked. "But it's a long story, too."

"Don't worry, I've got time," Lisa said. "Lots of it. I want to hear everything."

"Well . . ." Stevie began. She didn't leave out the slightest detail, from her first minute at the mall onward. By the time she got to the part about Phil's blue sweater, all three of the girls were laughing. Only Stevie could make such an embarrassing mistake seem so funny.

"Oh, I wish I'd been here to help you!" Lisa gasped between giggles.

"Thinking back on it, I'm not sure I needed help so much," Stevie replied. "After all, if you'd been there, you would have helped me find exactly the right dress, I would have fought with my mother like crazy to buy it, and then I would have been horribly out of place at the dance."

"Okay, so you didn't need help," Lisa said. "You did it all by yourself. If I'd been here to help I would have just made matters worse."

"No, the whole thing would have been a lot more fun," Stevie said.

"So, now, the dance?" Carole asked. She hadn't talked to Stevie since the dance and wanted all the details of the glamorous evening. Stevie supplied them.

"So what happened at midnight?" Lisa asked. "Did he kiss you? You're supposed to kiss at midnight, aren't you?" Lisa could have sworn Stevie blushed when she asked the question. When Lisa saw that, she knew. "Okay, so he did kiss you. It must have been a really good kiss, don't you think, Carole?"

Carole just laughed. Stevie did, too. "Sure it was,"

Stevie admitted. "But the funny thing about it was that I wasn't even paying much attention to him at the time."

"You weren't?" Carole asked. "Isn't that a little bit like not watching where you want your horse to go?"

Stevie looked at Lisa. "Only Carole would think of comparing kissing to riding!" she teased. Then she continued. "The funny thing about the kiss was that at midnight, I found myself thinking about you two. Remember when we promised we would? Well, I'd forgotten the promise, but I did it anyway."

"You know what?" Lisa said excitedly. Carole and Stevie looked at her. "There I was, more than a thousand miles away from you guys, in a world like you've never seen, under tropical starlight with the Caribbean lapping at the nearby beach, and at midnight, all I could think of was you two! How about you, Carole? Did it work for you, too?"

Carole nodded. "This isn't funny, this is weird. I was watching a movie with my father and all of a sudden, as the words *Happy New Year* crawled across the television screen, you two popped into my head. I think we can declare our ESP experiment a total success."

"I don't know that it was really ESP," Lisa said thoughtfully after a while. She was prone to thoughtful considerations. "Maybe it was just logic."

"How's that?" Stevie challenged her.

"Well, although you two spent some time together, the three of us have basically been separated for a whole week. We each had something difficult we had to do and we did it, but, for me at least, the whole time, all I kept thinking was how much I wanted you two to be there with me. See, thinking of you at midnight on New Year's Eve is really just an extension of that reality."

"*Extension of that reality?*" Stevie echoed. "Where'd you get that from?"

Lisa shrugged modestly. "I made it up," she said.

"Well, then I can make up the ESP thing. I like it a lot better," Stevie said.

"So do I," Lisa agreed.

"Me, too," Carole said. "And the really good thing about that is that if we ever have to be apart again, we have a way of being together in spite of it."

"An even better thing is if we never have to be apart again!" Stevie said.

"I'll drink to that," Lisa said, raising her soda can. "So, Happy New Year, Saddle Club!"

The cans clunked together for Lisa's toast. It was nice knowing that each of them could solve problems on her own. It was nicer to think that they didn't always have to.

ABOUT THE AUTHOR

BONNIE BRYANT is the author of more than forty books for young readers, including the best-selling novelizations of *The Karate Kid* movies and *Teenage Mutant Ninja Turtles* movie. The Saddle Club books are her first for Bantam Skylark. She wrote her first book eight years ago and has been busy at her word processor ever since. (For her first three years as an author, Ms. Bryant was also working in the office of a publishing company. In 1986, she left her job to write full-time.)

Whenever she can, Ms. Bryant goes horseback riding in her hometown, New York City. She's had many riding experiences in the city's Central Park that have found their way into her Saddle Club books—and lots which haven't!

The author has two sons, and they all live together in an apartment in Greenwich Village that is just too small for a horse.

THE SADDLE CLUB

A blue-ribbon series by Bonnie Bryant

Stevie, Carole and Lisa are all very different, but they *love* horses! The three girls are best friends at Pine Hollow Stables, where they ride and care for all kinds of horses. Come to Pine Hollow and get ready for all the fun and adventure that comes with being 13!

- [ ] 15594 HORSE CRAZY #1 ....$2.75
- [ ] 15611 HORSE SHY #2 ....$2.75
- [ ] 15626 HORSE SENSE #3 ....$2.75
- [ ] 15637 HORSE POWER #4 ....$2.75
- [ ] 15703 TRAIL MATES #5 .... $2.75
- [ ] 15728 DUDE RANCH #6 ....$2.75
- [ ] 15754 HORSE PLAY #7 ....$2.75
- [ ] 15769 HORSE SHOW #8 ....$2.75
- [ ] 15780 HOOF BEAT #9 ....$2.75
- [ ] 15790 RIDING CAMP #10 ....$2.75
- [ ] 15805 HORSE WISE #11 ....$2.75
- [ ] 15821 RODEO RIDER BOOK #12 ....$2.75
- [ ] 15832 STARLIGHT CHRISTMAS #13 ....$2.95
- [ ] 15847 SEA HORSE #14 ....$2.95

Watch for other SADDLE CLUB books all year. More great reading—and riding to come!

Buy them at your local bookstore or use this handy page for ordering.

Bantam Books, Dept. SK34, 414 East Golf Road, Des Plaines, IL 60016

Please send me the items I have checked above. I am enclosing $_____ (please add $2.50 to cover postage and handling). Send check or money order, no cash or C.O.D.s please.

Mr/Ms _____

Address _____

City/State _____ Zip _____

SK34-1/91

Please allow four to six weeks for delivery.
Prices and availability subject to change without notice.